# Jill's Gymkhana

'If anyone had told me three years ago that anything so terrific as a gymkhana would ever be associated with my name I should have thought them completely mad.'

This is Jill's introduction to the story of how she advances from being an 11-year-old girl without a pony or any knowledge of how to ride one, to a confident 14-year-old riding her own pony to success at the Chatton Show gymkhana.

Ruby Ferguson

# Jill's Gymkhana

*Illustrated by Bonar Dunlop*

 **KNIGHT BOOKS**

*the paperback division of Brockhampton Press*

ISBN 0 340 04136 6

*First Knight Books edition 1968*
*This edition first published 1970 by Knight Books,*
*the paperback division of Brockhampton Press Ltd, Leicester*
*Seventh impression 1974*

*Printed and bound in Great Britain by*
*Cox & Wyman Ltd, London, Reading and Fakenham*

*First published by Hodder and Stoughton Ltd 1949*
*Illustrations copyright © 1968 Brockhampton Press Ltd*

# Contents

# 1 - My dream

Just look at that title! You see, I am the Jill concerned, and quite honestly if anyone had told me three years ago that anything so terrific as a gymkhana would ever be associated with my name I should have thought them completely mad. Yet such was to be my destiny.

(That lovely phrase is not my own, I got it out of a library novel that Mummy is reading.)

I was only eleven, three years ago, when Mummy and I came to live at Pool Cottage, Chatton, and I quickly noticed that for all the children in that part of the world the one thing seemed to be riding. Every day I would hear the clop of many hoofs coming nearer, and I would rush to the window and see a riding school go by with a string of ponies ridden by children of all ages from six to sixteen.

So after a while I said, 'Oh, Mummy, do you think I could possibly have riding lessons? All the children here seem to ride.'

Mummy sighed, and then she said, 'Jill, I hate to have to, but you know what I'm going to say, don't you?'

'Yes,' I said. 'We can't afford it. O.K.'

And that was that.

Now before we go any further I had better say that if you are blasé about ponies you had better put this book down, because you will be infuriated to find that most of it is about a beginner, namely Me. And the same thing applies if you are one of those people who was practically born in the saddle; or if you ride nothing but blood ponies; or if you happen to be the fastest woman over timber in East Woldshire; or if your father buys all his horses at Tattersall's. It will be too simple for you. You see, my pony – but I'm going miles ahead.

When my father was alive we lived in a white house that was big and rambling, at the foot of a hill in Wales. Daddy didn't ride, but he loved horses above all animals. When we went out for a walk he would never pass a field with a horse in it, but he would call the horse and somehow it would come to him, and he would stroke its nose and talk to it, and it was almost as though he and the horse knew each other's language.

One day when my father was stroking a horse's nose a farmer came by and said, 'Look-you-now!' (Which is a Welsh way of saying Gosh.) The reason was that this particular horse was supposed to be a nasty creature that its owner couldn't do anything with. But my father could, and that was why the farmer said, 'Look-you-now!'

So I naturally grew up with the idea that horses were animals to be fond of, and Daddy promised that someday I should have riding lessons. But just about then he had to go to West Africa on business for his firm, and later we got a cable to say that he had fever. And he never came back to us.

Unfortunately there was very little money for Mummy and me, so Mummy sold our house and with what money she had she bought Pool Cottage at Chatton – which is quite a decent place really – and then she only had the little that was left and what she got from writing her children's books.

We had only just come to Chatton and our cottage was actually about two miles from the shops, and we didn't know anybody and it was still the summer holidays, so apart from helping Mummy with beds and dusting and things like that I hadn't much to do. Mummy did things in the house every morning and cooked the dinner; and after dinner she got out her typewriter and settled down to work while I just went out and meandered about.

Not very far from our cottage there was a farm, and next to the farm was a paddock, and in the paddock was a piebald pony. He was sturdy but graceful, about fourteen hands, with a nice action and a very intelligent face; but his mane and tail were ragged and he looked a bit out of condition. This wasn't surprising when I discovered from observation that he spent his entire life in that paddock and nobody ever exercised him, or even worked him, or seemed to bother with him at all.

One day when I was leaning over the gate, as I got into the habit of doing, I called the pony in the way Daddy used to call. He lifted his head from cropping and looked at me, but he didn't come. However I persevered, and at last he came up to within about two yards of me, looked at me in a puzzled way, and then with rather a disappointed expression turned away.

Of course! I ought to have brought him something. I rushed home, and shouted, 'Mummy! Can I take some lump sugar for a pony up the road?'

Mummy said, 'Oh, must you! I'm right in the middle of a sentence ... I don't think the farmers like you to give them sugar, dear, but there are some carrots in a bag in the scullery. Wash them first ... oh, I've forgotten how that sentence was going to end now!'

I took three of the best carrots, washed them under the tap, and went charging back to the paddock on my bike. I was quite excited when I hung over the gate and called to the pony. To my surprise he came at once, at a lovely trot. When he was about two yards away he stood still, as he had done before, but this time I held out my hand with the carrot placed temptingly on my open palm. His face lighted up, as you know ponies' faces do. He looked simply thrilled, and he came and took the carrot gently while his velvety lips brushed my hand. There he stood chewing, sublimely happy, and while he chewed I stroked his nose and cheeks.

Then I gave him the other two carrots, and said good-bye, and rode off on my bike. I nearly over-balanced looking back, and he was standing at the gate looking longingly after me.

After that Mummy simply never had a carrot left; I took them all for Patchy, as I called him. Of course I told her I had more or less adopted this pony, and that now he recognized me as soon as my bike hove in sight, and he would stop cropping grass and dash to the gate to meet me and the carrots.

I asked her, too, to see if she could find out anything about Patchy and why his owner left him alone in that paddock all day; and at last the milkman told us that Farmer Clay had taken the pony in payment of a bad debt, thinking that perhaps his daughter would like to ride, but the girl didn't care about riding – can you imagine? I could just picture the fat, stodgy thing! – so Farmer Clay being easy-going, Patchy just stayed in the paddock where he was and nobody bothered about him at all.

I went to see Patchy every day, sometimes twice, and the rest of the time, I just messed about and wished I knew somebody.

Then one day when I had reached the pony's gate I noticed that the farmer was in the paddock and was coming towards me. I thought perhaps he was angry, but he wasn't. He just said, 'Good day,' and I said, 'Good day,' and he said, 'You like the pony?' and I said, 'I should jolly well think I do.'

He said, 'I notice you've been round here a lot. That's a nice riding pony, well mannered and plenty of spirit. Just right for you. Why don't you ask your Ma to buy him for you?'

The idea gave me such a shock that I goggled at him like a fish.

'He'd make a jumper, he would, if he was trained,' said Farmer Clay. 'A grand little pony and no mistake. You just ask your Ma what about it.'

My head was spinning round by now at the very thought of being able to own Patchy.

'How – how much would he cost?' I stuttered.

Farmer Clay thought for a minute.

'Well, shall we say twenty-five pound? Twenty-five pound, and that's a bargain, I can tell you. But he's on my hands, as you might say.'

Of course he might as well have said twenty-five hundred, or even twenty-five thousand.

'Thanks very much,' I said. 'I think I'd better be going home now.'

'You ask your Ma like I said.'

'Yes,' I said. 'Yes, I will.'

But as soon as I had got away I realized that I wouldn't, because I had enough sense not to worry Mummy about something that was quite impossible. So I decided that I would never go and see Patchy again.

Four awful days went by. I didn't know what to do with the time, because I could only go to Chatton if I didn't want to pass Patchy's field, so I mooched about the

house, plunged in blackest gloom. Then one night Mummy, who was very noticing, said, 'Has anything happened to your friend the pony, Jill?'

'How do you mean?' I said, turning red.

'Only that my carrot bag is quite full. You haven't been to see Patchy for days. Now there *is* something the matter! Out with it.'

So I shrugged my shoulders, and then told her all. When I had finished she said, 'Poor Jill, I wish I could buy you the pony, you know I do. But twenty-five pounds! If I had that much money to spare I'd get the scullery floor relaid, or the garden dug over, and some apple trees put in, or a new roof for the hens, and the chimneys pointed, and –'

'I know, Mummy,' I said. 'It's O.K. But, oh *gosh*, if I could only have had Patchy! You see, he's used to being

out of doors and he could live in our orchard, and I'd
look after him and everything.'

'He'd cost a lot to feed, especially in the winter.'

'I thought of that,' I said. (Actually I'd thought of
everything in the silent watches of the night.) 'I thought
I might lend him to one of the riding schools to use, on
condition that they fed and stabled him in the winter.'

'You've never been taught to ride, Jill.'

'I could teach myself.'

'It isn't as easy as you think, and riding lessons are
expensive.'

'Perhaps they would let me work at the riding school,
mucking out stables and so on, in return for riding
lessons?'

Mummy shook her head.

'You know it's all impossible. Why are we talking
about it? Oh dear, I wish you could have got interested
in *anything* else but horses.'

## 2 - Black Boy

I EXPECT you have found out that life, usually so humdrum and school-dinner-ish, occasionally has magic spasms.

A few mornings later I was in the kitchen making the coffee for breakfast when I heard Mummy go to the door to meet the postman.

Suddenly she called out, 'Oh! Oh!' in an excited voice, so I went running and saw her standing at the door with a letter open in her hand.

'Oh, Jill!' she cried, 'what do you think? My agent has sold the serial rights of *The Little House of Smiles* and has sent me a cheque for seventy-five guineas. Seventy-five guineas that I never expected. And it's the very first of my stories ever to be serialized. I can hardly believe it!'

I could hardly believe it either, because frankly I always thought that *The Little House of Smiles* was quite the most revolting of Mummy's books. It was about a rather sickening little boy called Terry, who worked with his grandmother making smiles and packing them into cardboard boxes to send to people who hadn't any.

So I just said, 'Nice work, Mummy.'

While we were eating our breakfast she said, 'Seventy-eight pounds and seventy-five pence. I'm going to spend it on things we need. I shall get the scullery floor relaid, and the chimneys pointed, and maybe the hen house properly repaired, and I should *like* to buy a new gas cooker –'

'Yes, Mummy,' I said.

'Oh, Jill,' she said, '*you* shall have some of it for your very own, to buy what you like. I know it's extravagant and we can't afford it, but life can't be all pinching and scraping or there isn't any joy left. I'll give you – thirty pounds for your own.'

I nearly passed out.

'Thirty pounds! Mummy! Oh crumbs!'

And then we both had the same thought.

'Oh, Mummy!' I cried. 'Can I? Can I have Patchy?'

'I think we're a bit mad,' she said, 'but I suppose you can, *if* you can feed him and care for him properly.'

So that very morning, after Mummy had been to the bank, I went along to Farmer Clay's and told him what I had never thought I should be able to tell him, that Mummy said I could buy Patchy for twenty-five pounds.

'Right!' he said cheerfully. 'He'll win you a lot of prizes, that pony will. Want to take him now?'

'Oh, yes, please,' I said.

So he brought Patchy from the paddock, and he said, 'Wait a minute,' and disappeared into the stable, and the next minute he came out carrying a saddle and bridle.

'I'll throw these in,' he said. 'They're a bit shabby but they'll do till you get something better.'

I was thrilled, because until then I hadn't even thought of tack and what it would cost me to buy it.

'What about fodder?' asked Farmer Clay. 'Shall I let you have some to be going on with?'

'Oh, what does he eat?' I asked.

'You'll want oats, bran, and chaff. See this measure? Give him about one and a half of oats, the same of bran, and a double handful of chaff. Mix it well together.'

So after Farmer Clay had put on Patchy's snaffle-bridle and saddle I paid him for the pony and the fodder.

'Patchy,' I said, patting my own pony for the first time, 'Patchy darling, you're mine.'

'Do you call him Patchy?' said the farmer. 'His real name's Black Boy.'

'I like that better,' I said.

'Well, up you get,' said Farmer Clay.

I went scarlet, because I had never mounted a pony; but he didn't notice, and with a laugh he picked me up under his arm and placed me in the saddle.

The next moment I found myself riding – actually riding – down the lane. But it wasn't a bit like I thought it was going to be; I felt all wrong, and didn't know what to do with my hands and legs, and I went joggety-jog, and felt as though I was going to slip right over Black Boy's neck. And I simply prayed that he wouldn't break into a trot! But he walked along quite sedately and we got home at last.

Mummy was waiting at the gate.

'He's lovely,' she said. 'When you're tired of riding him, let's put him in the orchard and see how he likes it.'

'We'll put him in right away,' I said, 'while I find some bins for his fodder' – unfastening the bags which Farmer Clay had tied to the saddle.

But now I'm ashamed to say I was faced with a new difficulty. I didn't know how to unsaddle my pony and I didn't like to tell Mummy; so I fumbled about for ages while Black Boy looked at me in a surprised sort of way, and I'm sure I pinched him and thumped him though he was incredibly patient, and at last I got his wretched saddle off and the bridle too, though I couldn't imagine how I was ever going to get them on again.

In the afternoon I had a try, and a sorry mess I made of it. First I put the snaffle bit in his mouth, and then he spat

It out, and then I tried to push his face into the cheek bands, and I simply won't go on with the sorry tale, for in the end Mummy came out to help and with her common sense and my brute force we got my pony more or less ready for me to mount.

I said mount, but it was a scramble rather than a mount. In the end even Black Boy lost his patience and walked off, with me as it were hanging between heaven and earth. I landed in the grass with a thud, and Mummy giggled like anything. So she helped me up, and caught Black Boy, and then she did what Farmer Clay had done and lifted me bodily into the saddle.

'Sit up straight,' she said.

So I rode up and down the lane outside our cottage most of the afternoon; at least when I say 'rode' I mean that my pony walked a bit and, realizing that he could do anything he liked, stopped to crop grass, while I just sat there like a sack of potatoes, having no control over him whatsoever.

He started when he liked and he stopped when he liked; I was as bad as that. I pulled on the reins, as if I were trying my weight, and if Black Boy started I flattered myself that it was my doing, not realizing that the poor thing was just trying to escape from this murderous woman who was jagging at his mouth. When I wanted him to stop I tugged away again, but it didn't stop him. He just arched his neck and rolled his eyes, and the next minute I was off and he was several yards away.

I am telling you this disgraceful story to show you how hopeless I was, in case anyone who reads this book is hopeless too. Of course if any hard woman to hounds has read thus far she will now be scarlet with rage and exasperation and probably trying to get me prosecuted.

But nobody could have been more disappointed than I was that first day I owned a pony. Riding had looked so easy when I saw the other children doing it. But you know how it is. I once went to Wimbledon and saw people play in the Lawn Tennis Championships, and the balls literally seemed to come right on to their rackets every time, so they couldn't have missed them if they tried. But when *you* try to do it, it doesn't work out that way at all. And it's the same with riding.

The next day, too, I was so stiff with using muscles that I didn't know I had that I just tottered about the house, and made a valiant attempt to laugh at myself as much as Mummy was laughing at me.

But inwardly I was feeling pretty low.

'Oh gosh!' I thought. 'It isn't any use without riding lessons, and I'm never going to afford any. It will take everything I've got – and more – just to buy fodder for Black Boy, especially in the winter.'

But I wasn't going to worry about the future, when I had been so marvellously lucky as to get a pony at all; so I went jogging on, day after day, getting more used to the feel of riding, but doing everything wrong, and not knowing how to make Black Boy do the things I wanted him to do.

# 3 - The Gymkhana

ONE day I saw a notice that there was to be a children's pony gymkhana the following Saturday, and I decided to go. I came away from that gymkhana sadder if not much wiser, after seeing quite small children doing the most marvellous things on ponies and riding them with a technique which left me gasping. But I'm going too far ahead.

I landed at the field on my bike a few minutes after two o'clock, and after buying an ice-cream I found a small gap at the side of the ring and worked my way in. All around me was green grass and blue sky, and wherever my eye roved it fell upon the noble Horse, which made me feel happy.

Judging was going on for the best rider under fourteen. There were twelve children in this event and they all looked frightfully good to me, as I gazed at them with the critical and envious eye of a pony-owner. They mounted and dismounted with perfect ease, ran beside their ponies, displayed a walk, trot, and canter, did a figure of eight, and unsaddled in about three swift, deft movements. I wriggled my toes inside my shoes, remembering my own awful struggles.

The first place went to a girl of about twelve on a grey pony, and I saw from my programme that she was called Susan Pyke and her pony was called Dear Arab. The second place went to a boy and the third to another girl.

I was very interested when the stewards began to erect the jumps for the first jumping event, which was under-twelves. There were five jumps, a box-hedge, a gate, a wall, a stile, and finally a triple bar, and they all looked mountainous to me, though looking back from my present experienced state I suppose they were about two-foot-six actually.

Then a voice from the amplifier said, 'All competitors for the under-twelve jumping in the ring, please,' and about fourteen children rode in on very keen-looking ponies. They rode their ponies up to each of the jumps in turn and let them see over the other side; then the ring was cleared and the first competitor came in.

She was only about ten and very nervous. Her pony refused at the first jump, and then jumped too late and brought wads of the hedge down. People laughed and the girl looked hot and worried. At the second jump her pony caught his hind feet and brought everything clattering down, and at the third he refused three times and was disqualified. I felt so sorry for the girl, especially when nobody clapped as she rode off except two fat ladies with bulgy handbags who I expect were her mother and her aunt.

Then a boy of about my age rode in and took the first three jumps marvellously; but, as you know, some ponies are so surprised by their own success that they lose their heads and begin bucking and fly-catching, and that is what this one did. He had two refusals at each of the last two jumps and knocked them both down as well, and the judge said, 'Fourteen faults.'

The next was the girl called Susan Pyke who had won first place in the riding event, and she really did jump beautifully. I was wild with envy. It was like one of those radio quizzes where they ask you who, if not yourself, you would wish to be, and at that moment I would have given anything to be Susan Pyke. How, with the general queerness of life, I came to alter my opinion this book will tell you, if you have the patience to go on with it. I expect at this moment you are saying, 'Well, of all the feeble ways to describe a gymkhana – I' Yes, it is feeble, and I was feeble, and that is why I am telling you all frightfully feeble ideas.

Everybody had to be a beginner once, even an M.F.H. though it is hard to imagine it. What I mean to say is, however exalted and beefy a person you may be in the equestrian world, you ought to be jolly humble. Because if you are not something usually happens to you that makes you feel lower than the worms. I am thinking of a boy I once encountered at a show who was telling everybody how demeaning it was for him to be riding in such a squalid gymkhana when he was really used to places like Richmond or even Wembley. While saying this he took a practice jump over a hurdle and his girth actually broke, and he soared through the air and landed where some of the Fat Cattle had been. And you know what Fat Cattle are like at shows.

So though now I am a person of wide experience and some knowledge of horsemanship I try not to be superior even to people who are very young and stand round the rails in cotton frocks looking envious. I expect you think this is just an awful lot of preaching, so I will continue with my story.

The girl called Susan Pyke finished her round with only two faults, and in the end she won first prize for this event, the second and third prizes being won by boys with three and three and a half faults respectively. I was so dumb that I didn't even know how faults were reckoned.

The under-sixteen jumping which followed was much more exciting, as the jumps were raised to three feet and the competitors were more experienced. After a while, even I could tell which ponies were going to jump well, for though full of spirit they had common sense as well which showed in their lovely but steady eyes. The 'silly' ponies turned out to be no good at all, and either refused the jumps or jumped too soon or too late.

Of course some of the faults were due to the riders' bad horsemanship; they were not in absolute harmony with their ponies. It was obvious to even an onlooker like me that rider and pony had to have complete understanding of each other and confidence in each other before their jumping could be successful.

The first prize-winner was a thin girl with a long plait, and though handicapped by wearing glasses which glittered in the sun, she had a most skilful way of holding her pony in until the split second before he had to jump, then letting him go, giving him a business-like Hup! and putting him over like a bird.

It was interesting to hear the onlookers' comments, and I listened hard because I wanted to learn.

There was one boy who soared up into the air at every jump, which knowing no better I thought looked very distinguished. He practically stood in his stirrups in mid-air, and then came back into the saddle with a bang. After this had happened twice, at the third jump the pony refused, once, twice, and a third time. The boy looked very crestfallen, for he was now disqualified and had to ride off the field.

'Do you blame the pony!' exclaimed a voice near me.

I looked round, and to my amazement realized that I was being addressed by a nice-looking man with a jolly face. He wasn't really ancient either, but somewhere about Mummy's age which was thirty-five.

'Why did he refuse?' I said, too interested to be shy or to remember putting-off things like not talking to strangers. 'I thought he was doing frightfully well.'

'If you were a pony,' he said, 'how would you like to have a great lump of boy crashed down on your back every time you jumped? The pony can't say he's had enough; he can only show it by a flat refusal to jump any more. You'd wonder where and by whom some of these people were taught. I hope the lad isn't your brother, by the way!'

'Oh no, I don't know him,' I said. 'But I thought he was riding very well, and I wished I could do it, until the pony refused.'

'Don't you ever ride yourself?' he asked.

'I've got a pony,' I said, 'but it isn't the same thing.'

After the jumping came Musical Chairs which I thought was the best game I had ever seen.

The chairs were placed in a circle in the middle of the ring, and the competitors cantered cautiously round the outside of the ring until the music stopped playing. Then they had to dismount and rush to a chair pulling their ponies with them.

Some of the ponies knew the game well, and it was an education to me to see the way those children dismounted, simply flying out of their saddles.

The final tussle was between a boy and a girl who both dashed at the last chair together and fell in a heap while everybody laughed loudly; but when the judge picked them up the girl was underneath and actually hanging on to the chair, so she was the winner and the boy was second.

'What did you mean,' asked my new friend suddenly, 'when you said that having a pony wasn't the same thing as riding?'

And then, to my own amazement, because I don't usually chatter to strangers, I found myself telling him the whole story of Black Boy. He seemed terribly interested.

'I say!' he said. 'You'll have to learn to ride.'

'Well, I've got a few ideas this afternoon,' I said, 'but I feel frightfully discouraged because when I try to do things myself it won't be half so easy as it seems to those children.'

'How would it be,' he said, 'if I came round to your place one afternoon to see your pony? I might be able to help you a bit.'

'Oh,' I said, 'do you ride?'

'I did,' he said; and then for the first time I noticed that he was actually sitting in a wheel chair and his legs were covered with a rug.

I looked embarrassed, but he gave a smile.

'My legs don't act any more,' he said. 'Isn't it a swindle? You see, I was careless enough to fall out of a plane. By the way, my name's Martin Lowe.'

'Mine's Jill Crewe,' I said, 'and I live at Pool Cottage in Pool Lane. I'd be frightfully glad if you'd come round and see me ride – or try to – and so would Mummy.'

'Then that's all arranged,' he said. 'What's the next thing? Oh, the bending.'

The bending race consisted of riding in and out of lines of poles. It was really skilful because I could see that a child had to make her pony turn or 'bend' as close to the

pole as possible so as not to lose distance. I couldn't
imagine how this was done, as I told my new friend.

'Watch how a child uses his legs and reins,' said he,
'and you'll soon get the idea. As he turns to the left he
presses with his right leg and heel to keep the pony's
quarters from swinging too far to the right and so losing
his balance.'

From this I guessed that Martin Lowe knew what he
was talking about.

Susan Pyke got the first prize in the bending race, and
the second was a boy who had not won before.

I could not imagine a greater thrill in life than to receive one of the coloured rosettes to fasten on my pony's
browband, and then to gallop round the ring with a
certificate in my teeth. It must be heaven, I thought.

'I believe you're envious,' said Martin Lowe.

'Yes I am,' I said, 'mad with envy. But I couldn't do it in a million years.'

'Of course you could,' he said rather sharply. 'These children you see winning prizes were not born on a pony's back. Two years ago some of them had never been in a saddle. But they *learned*, and I tell you it means work. Of course you can do it, you can do anything if you're patient and obedient and willing to learn and don't get the idea that you're marvellous as soon as you can make a pony obey your aids. We'll see!'

# 4 - Martin

A DAY or two later I was idling about in the lane on Black Boy when to my horror I heard the sound of approaching hoofs and along came the riding school with their master, all at a beautiful collected trot. (I didn't know then that it was a collected trot, but I knew it looked right and whatever I was doing looked wrong.) I couldn't get out of the way; and just at that moment too, Black Boy chose to ignore my feeble rein-pulling and put down his head to crop grass.

All the children stared at me as they passed, and I recognized the girl called Susan Pyke who had done so well in the gymkhana. She gave me a scornful look, and then said something to her nearest neighbour, and they both started laughing. That set the others off, and even the riding master grinned and cast me a look full of superciliousness and disdain.

I felt myself go hot and red and my hands and feet felt enormous. When they had all gone by I knew I wouldn't have any more pleasure from my pony that day. I slid off his back in my usual awkward fashion and led him home, and then I went up to my room and sat on the bed and howled like a kid for ages. Because the most shattering thing in the world is being laughed at.

And then I thought, 'Oh, Jill, you are the most awful idiot. Fancy crying because you can't ride! When all you've got to do is to learn how, like Martin Lowe said. If other people can, you can.'

But these thoughts only made me howl still more, because Martin Lowe seemed to have forgotten his promise to come and see my pony.

I suppose I should have stayed there for hours, sniffing away in the silly way one does when one is only eleven, but I heard Mummy calling me down, so I washed my face and hoped she wouldn't notice anything.

'Oh, Jill,' she said when I came down, 'I'm so frightfully busy with my new chapter. Do you think you could possibly make the tea today?'

So I started to cut sandwiches and spread them with chopped lettuce and cucumber, and that made me feel better as honest toil always does.

The very next morning, which was Saturday, as I was finishing the dismal daily task of making my bed, I happened to glance out of the window and there was Martin Lowe wheeling himself in at our gate in his chair.

I made one wild dish downstairs and met him at the door.

'Oh, I thought you were never coming,' I said.

'Did you mind so much?' he said. 'I'm very sorry if it seemed a long time. I caught a chill at the gymkhana – sounds feeble, but there it is – and had to stay in bed for a few days. But now I'm here and I want to see that pony.'

I introduced him to Mummy, and then we all went out to the orchard. I was feeling rather worried, wondering whether Black Boy would deign to come when I called him. Lately, realizing that I was a pretty hopeless person, he had begun to play me up and would give me a cheeky look from his soft black eye, as much as to say, 'Come and make me do it, if you can!'

So I led the way to the orchard with my fingers crossed,

and wondering if I could summon up a loud commanding tone.

There was my pony, swishing his tail gently under the farthest apple tree. He looked up with surprise when he saw three of us coming, and I think it was curiosity which fetched him rather than my plaintive cry. Anyway, he came, and I felt like saying, 'Thank goodness.'

Black Boy took no notice of me, his lawful owner, but walked straight up to Martin Lowe and began to nuzzle him gently, as much as to say, 'I can tell you know some-

thing about horses, which is more than these people do.'

Martin called him a good boy, and examined his feet and his mouth, and his eyes and coat.

'He's a grand pony,' said Martin at last, 'and if he has no real faults I consider he was a bargain at twenty-five pounds. Now you have to school him and bring out the best in him. I say! He's not very clean, is he? How often do you groom him?'

This was awful. I went as red as a beetroot.

'I don't know how to,' I said.

'You've got a dandy brush, I suppose?'

'No,' I muttered. 'I don't know what it is.'

'Well, you must get one today,' was all that Martin said, 'and tomorrow I'll come and show you how to use it. You'll need a water brush too, and a body brush and a curry-comb, and a stable rubber for finishing off. If you go to Wilks' the saddler and say I sent you, you'll be given the right things.'

'Will they cost a lot?' I blurted out, and then shut my eyes as I caught Mummy's eye.

'Look here,' said Martin, 'there's no point in you buying those things when we've got loads of them knocking about at home. I'll bring a set round tomorrow, and then when Black Boy gets really well groomed you might buy him a set of his own for a birthday present. There's no actual hurry. Will that do?'

'Oh, it's frightfully good of you!' I gasped, and Mummy looked relieved and yet doubtful, as grown-ups do when they think they are being done favours to.

'Meanwhile, where are your saddle and bridle?'

'In the kitchen,' I said. 'I'll fetch them.'

I rushed and got them, and Martin said, 'Well, they could be cleaned too, couldn't they?'

This was kind, as they were actually filthy. I hadn't even noticed before. Once more I could have died.

'Never mind now,' said Martin. 'Stick them on the pony.'

'I – I don't really know how,' I muttered.

'Don't know *how*! But how have you managed –'

'Oh, just anyhow,' I growled. 'All wrong.'

'Well, show me how you've been doing it.'

Oh dear, how awful my efforts must have looked to Martin.

'Stop!' he said, and though he sat all the time in a wheel chair I assure you he could be very commanding.

'Stop, Jill, for heaven's sake. That poor pony! He must have the patience of an angel to put up with you, hurting his ears and mouth, and pinching his skin and pulling his girths too tight. I wonder he could breathe. Now we'll begin from the beginning. First speak gently to your pony and slip the reins over his head and neck. Then stand close to his head and pass your right arm round and under, taking hold of the crownpiece of the bridle with your right hand and the bit with your left. Now put his offside ear – that's the offside one, duffer – between the crownpiece and browband, and slip your left thumb into the side of his mouth. In goes the bit; now put the other ear through – there! Could anything be easier?'

'Oh!' I said.

'Now for the saddle. First run the stirrups up the leathers or they will smack your pony and annoy him. I bet you've annoyed him lots of times. Now fling your saddle on as deftly as you can and fasten the girths, but you must be able to insert three fingers, and run them down so that the flesh isn't wrinkled underneath. That's better. Now let me see you mount.'

I did my best, and Martin said, 'Oh dear! What a scramble. You look as though you're climbing a wall.'

'Well, tell me how,' I said.

'Stand with your back to Black Boy's head. Take the reins in your left hand and place it on his withers, just in front of the saddle. Now take hold of the saddle with your right hand and place your left foot in the stirrup – no, right up to the instep, please. Now spring! Spring, I said, not lumber up. Bring both feet together, over with your right leg, and sit down gently. That wasn't too bad at all. Now get down and do it all over again.'

It was like a dream, I couldn't believe it. I was having a riding lesson.

I suppose to some of you this will sound absolutely pathetic, but I told you I was going to describe things from the very beginning and the very beginning for me was when I learned to mount my pony properly.

'I gather you're not very good at dismounting,' Martin was saying.

'Not what *you'd* call dismounting,' I murmured, wondering how much lower I was going to fall in the way of shame and abasement.

'Well, look here,' he said, 'even at gymkhanas you'll see a lot of very slack and careless dismounting. People often just free their stirrups and slither off. You can't afford to do that until you're a very experienced rider, and know when the judge's eye is on you and when you can afford to take liberties with technique. Here and now you've got to learn to do it properly every time.'

And he proceeded to tell me what your baby sister of four probably knows, about bringing the right foot over to the left foot, standing straight for a second, then freeing the left foot and jumping neatly down. He made me do this a good many times.

'Can you stand any more?' said Martin. 'Because for one thing, your stirrup leathers are the wrong length. Come here ... there! Try that,' he added after he had directed me from his chair how to shorten my leathers.

We then had a very earnest twenty minutes while he

told me how to sit in the saddle and what to do with my hands, and the right position for my feet and knees.

I expect you are bored stiff with all this, but there isn't going to be much more of it. I wasn't bored at the time, but Black Boy was and he began to show it unmistakably.

'Black Boy's looking at me with a "Save me" look in his eye,' said Mummy laughing.

'I could go on for ever,' I said.

'Mr Lowe couldn't,' said Mummy. 'He's already getting the wild and desperate look of one who has reached the end of his tether.'

'Not a bit of it!' said Martin, quite indignantly. 'But all the same I think we'd better finish for today. Jill has got enough to practise.'

'It's most awfully good of you,' said Mummy, 'to help her like this. We don't know how to thank you, do we, Jill?'

'Well, don't thank me for coming,' said Martin, 'because that's the last thing I want. I've thoroughly enjoyed myself. It's grand to think I'm doing something useful. You see, for ages I haven't been any use at all, since I couldn't walk, and it was getting me down. If I can teach somebody to ride it will buck me up no end. So if you'll let me come again, that's all I ask.'

I was wildly happy all the evening, and made such a noise about it that Mummy had to get annoyed with me, which she rarely does over simple things like making a noise.

I expect you think it was a lot of fuss about nothing, especially if you were born in the saddle and photographed with your nurse holding you up when hounds met on your ancestral lawn.

But as the week-end wore on I quietened down quite a lot, for a black day loomed before me on the following Tuesday.

# 5 – School

THE horrid truth was that the summer holidays were over and it was the first day of school. And what was worse, my first day at a new school, The Pines School for Girls, in Chatton.

At nine-thirty on that grim morning I was standing in the headmistress's room, feeling very clean and stiff in my new school uniform of fawn blouse and brown tunic, and trying to stop my new shoes from squeaking.

'You are Jill Crewe?' said Miss Grange-Dudley. 'Let me see, on the results of the entrance examination we have placed you in the Lower Third form. The average age there, I see, is eleven years and five months. How old are you?'

'Eleven years and – and – seven months,' I said, doing some violent mental arithmetic.

'Then you will have to work very hard, Jill, since you are above rather than below the average,' said Miss Grange-Dudley with a head-mistressy smile.

(I had an awful time trying not to giggle, because I thought of a story of Daddy's, about a man in a hotel who said to a little page boy, 'What is the average tip you get here?' The boy replied, 'Twenty pence, sir,' so the man said, 'Very well, here is twenty pence for you.' And the boy said, 'Oh thank you, sir! You're the only gentleman who has ever come up to the average.')

Miss Grange-Dudley then pressed a bell, and a girl of

about sixteen came in, wearing glasses and a prefect's badge.

'Oh, Marguerite, this is Jill Crewe, a new girl for the Lower Third. Please take her along to the form-room and hand her over to Miss Wright.'

So I followed Marguerite, who was in the sixth form, along a corridor and up a flight of stairs, all smelling of floor polish and chalk and blackboards; and she tapped at a door and in we went. I felt as though a thousand eyes were fixed upon me, though actually there were thirty girls and the form mistress.

'A new girl for you, Miss Wright,' said Marguerite. 'Jill Crewe.'

'Oh, good morning, Jill,' said Miss Wright, who was rather old and very thin. 'That is your desk, on the second row. Please sit quietly until we finish our *dictée*.'

Then she went on, '*Chaque jour la petite Marie et son frère* –', and I looked round to see if there was anyone I knew. On the front row was Susan Pyke; I didn't recognize anyone else.

After the *dictée* we had books and exercise books given out, and then it was break. All the girls streamed out of the room without taking any notice of me, so I followed them into the garden. Everybody was talking in excited groups except for a few miserable new girls who like myself hung about alone, so I went and sat on a bench beside a hedge.

Presently I heard some girls talking on the other side of the hedge.

A voice said, 'Have you seen the new girl in our form? It's that awful kid who has come to live at the cottage in Pool Lane.'

'Why awful?' said somebody else.

I screwed myself round and peeped through a gap in the hedge. Susan Pyke was holding forth to several other girls who were all laughing.

'Well, the other day we passed her; she was riding on a pony, lolling all over it. Her stirrup-leathers were too long and her legs stuck straight out in front of her, and she had her hands somewhere up under her chin like Fido begging for a bone.'

'Oh, Susan, you are a scream!'

'And if you'd *seen* how she was dressed! An absolute sight! Frightful old jeans, no hat, and actually *sandals*.'

'No! Not really! How awful.'

I went home at lunch-time absolutely blazing. You see, up to then I had never bothered much about what I wore, but now I wondered why I could have been so blind. All the children I had seen on their ponies had, of course, worn lovely light-coloured jodhpurs or breeches, and neat tailored riding coats, and hard hats or crash caps and string gloves. I knew perfectly well that those clothes must cost a lot of money, and that I could never have them. I wasn't even going to ask Mummy for them because it would only worry her. I realized that getting Black Boy was only the beginning of the expense and perhaps it was a pity I had ever bought him.

You can guess I felt pretty grim and low.

Mummy said, 'Well? How was school?'

'Oh, all right,' I said. But she must have noticed that I was rather silent during lunch because she kept looking at me in a thoughtful way.

I went back to afternoon school and got through it somehow, and came home to tea.

Then Mummy said, 'What's the matter, Jill? What's happened?'

'Oh, nothing,' I said.

We had scarcely finished tea when I saw Martin Lowe's wheel chair coming in at the gate. I felt nearly too depressed to welcome him, but when he started laying things out on the table, I got interested in spite of myself.

'What's this for?' I asked, picking up a curry-comb.

'That is actually to fetch the dirt out of the body-brush,' said Martin, 'but you're beginning at the wrong end. The first tool to get familiar with is this one, the dandy-brush. You see it is stiff, and with it you will brush Black Boy all over, working towards his tail, getting out the dirt with a circular movement but always finishing your stroke the way the hair lies. You brush his tail with that one too. Next you use the damp water-brush; then you rub him over with the body-brush, cleaning it out as you go with the curry-comb. Finally you put on a shine with a wisp of hay and finish off with a clean stable-rubber. Here are all your tools; now let's go out and groom Black Boy.'

He sat in his wheel chair, and under his instructions I made the best job I could of grooming my pony for the first time. I was jolly clumsy over it, but I did try, and when I had finished Black Boy shone like patent leather, even if it was a bit patchy, and I made up my mind I would always keep him like that.

'Now let's see if you remember what we learned on Saturday,' said Martin. 'Show me how you saddle, mount, and dismount from your pony. And remember that in putting on saddle and bridle your first concern ought to be your pony's comfort. Always take time and trouble over it, and never put anything on in a slapdash way.'

Martin then praised me for the improvement I had made, and suggested that we should go into the lane so that he could see me actually riding.

'My hands still feel wrong,' I said, thinking of the loathsome Susan Pyke.

'They're all right. Keep them low, with your elbows close to your sides.'

'How tight should I hold the reins?'

'Well, that's important. The reins are definitely *not* something to hang on to for the purpose of keeping your balance. All you have to do is to keep a light feel of your pony's mouth, and so establish contact. It's balance, balance all the time. Now show me how you walk – sit straight – straighter than that. Good! You look very nice, Jill, if you can maintain that position.'

His words of praise made me feel a bit better, after my

hideous humiliation of the morning. What rankled me was that it had all been true, what Susan Pyke had said, and I *had* looked awful and it had been my own fault. But at least no one should ever be able to say that I rode badly again.

However my pride was shortly to be brought down a peg or two. Martin kept saying, 'Walk! Walk!' and I walked and walked Black Boy up and down the lane while he looked on critically.

'I'm sick of walking,' I said at last. 'Can't I do something else?'

'You can do anything you like,' said Martin.

So I used my heels on Black Boy in a way that I considered smart and horsemanlike, and off he went at a trot with me bouncing about all over the place. As I found this very uncomfortable, I pressed him to a canter, hoping for the best, and eventually finished up more or less on his neck.

'I suppose that looked pretty awful,' I said to Martin. 'I'm really beginning to wonder if Black Boy's pace is right for me.'

'I suppose one excuse is as good as another,' he said.

'Black Boy *always* takes off on the wrong foot,' I said.

'How unfortunate,' said Martin in a maddening sort of way.

'Well, what can I do about it?' I said.

'I shouldn't trot or canter until you've learned to walk,' he said kindly. 'I'll give you some tips next time I come, and now it looks to me as though that pony has had enough, so let's go and rub him down before it gets too dark. Remember, a good rider always puts his horse's comfort before his own, and however tired and hungry you may be after a ride, Jill, your pony must be attended to and fed before you go for your own bath and grub.'

I resolved to do quite a lot of practising before Martin came again, so as not to make any more exhibitions of myself and my incompetence. Then Mummy came out and asked Martin whether he would like to stay to supper.

'It's only a gipsy supper of roast potatoes and cheese,' she said, but Martin seemed pleased to be asked.

Round the table he began to talk to us. It seemed that before he had his crash in the R.A.F. he had kept three riding horses and had taken many prizes with them at shows and gymkhanas. Now he was living with his parents who were rather old and fussy. His mother was always pitying him and telling him to rest and take care, which was really the worst thing for anybody like Martin, and his father was apt to say, 'I've just been looking at all the cups you won in the old days, tch, tch, tch!' Which was cruel, though not meant to be.

We tried to eat roast potatoes politely as we had a guest, but it was difficult, and soon we were all laughing and scooping them out with spoons in our usual carefree way. Martin seemed pleased rather than horrified. Then we had baked apples, the middles stuffed with sultanas and brown sugar, and coffee made in the Cona, which I always do myself.

Martin promised to come again on Saturday afternoon, and meanwhile I was to practise all I had learned. However when I got to bed I couldn't sleep for thinking about having the wrong clothes and never being able to get the right ones. But perhaps I could do something better than jeans and sandals!

I knew jodhpurs cost the earth. I had only one pound fifty which Black Boy would soon eat up; but after school next day I went and gazed in a few shop windows, and finally my eye lit on some quite decent-looking bluey-grey denims which were marked seventy-five pence.

I thought a bit, and then recklessly plunged and bought a pair. I dashed home on my bike and flew up to my room. I dug out an old white cotton shirt that was quite plain and put it on, with the grey denims. Then I put on my school tie which was fawn, brown, and green in stripes and my school hat which was plain brown felt turned up all round, and my tie-up brown shoes. I didn't look too bad at all; I was neat and sporting, anyhow, not sloppy.

I went down and had some milk and buns – Mummy was working hard that afternoon – and then I saddled Black Boy and rode him up and down the lane a bit. I felt much smarter and more of a rider. Even hating The Pines school seemed a bit less violent now; and I dashed in whistling, and made a cup of tea and took it in to Mummy who was very grateful.

# 6 - My friend Ann

THE next morning at break, to my surprise a girl came up and spoke to me. She looked rather nice, with curly red hair and a lot of freckles.

'I'm Ann Derry,' she said.

I had noticed her in the form-room, of course.

'Would you like to walk round with me?' she asked, and I said I would. It was a pleasant change having somebody to talk to instead of the stony silence which is often a new girl's fate.

I wondered why Ann, who seemed quite a popular girl, had bothered with me, but she explained, 'You see, Susan Pyke seems to have her knife into you for some reason. I loathe Susan Pyke, and therefore anybody that Susan Pyke loathes, I like, if you know what I mean.'

'It's mouldy being a new girl,' I said, 'but I'll probably survive. The worst of it is, I don't know anybody in Chatton, and all the other new girls seem to know each other.'

'I'll tell you what,' said Ann, 'would you like to sit by me in class instead of where you are? I'll ask Miss Wright if you can change desks with Marjorie Miles. Marjorie won't mind, in fact she'd rather have your desk because it is next to Diana Bush whom she has rather a crush on.'

The next day Ann invited me to go home to tea with her. When we arrived, we did our hair and washed, and then Ann's mother came in and said, 'Who is this little girl, dear?' which I thought was rather a lowering thing

42

to say, and I would have slain Mummy if she had said it to a friend of mine.

Ann went a bit red, and said, 'It's Jill Crewe, Mummy. I *told* you.'

We went down to the dining-room where tea was laid with a lace cloth and silver dishes as though for a grown-up party, and there were Ann's two little sisters, Pam and Brenda, clutching dolls and being shy. I just said, 'Hullo,' and they looked as if they were going to cry. They were all right really, only much too young to bother with. We had a lovely tea, with sardine sandwiches and tarts and iced cake. Mrs Derry kept saying things like, 'You've only had *two* sandwiches, darling. You must have three before any cake. Oh dear, oh dear, Pam is hardly eating *anything*. Do you feel ill, Pam darling? Brenda, you've been running about and getting too hot, I'm sure you have! Ann, you're not chewing your food twenty times, darling, and you know what Doctor Brown said.'

However this was over at last, and Mrs Derry said, 'Now take Jill to see your pony, dear.'

'Oh!' I said. 'I didn't know you had a pony.'

'Of course she has a pony,' said Mrs Derry. 'But she isn't a bit keen. I simply can't understand it. When I was her age I was riding and schooling my pony half the day long, and yet Ann has to be *driven* to go near Seraphine.'

'Oh, don't fuss so, Mummy,' said Ann.

'Well, we'll go to the stable,' said Mrs Derry; so off we went.

Seraphine – which I thought was rather a putting-off name anyway – was a lovely pony, grey, of about thirteen hands. She was beautifully groomed, but I learned that Mr Derry's handyman did that.

'I couldn't bother with anything like that,' said Ann.

'Actually, it's quite fun,' I said.

'Have you got a pony?' said Ann, surprised.

So I told her about Black Boy and how keen I was.

'There!' said Mrs Derry. 'I'm sure you'll do Ann a lot of good, Jill. Darling, *don't* stand so near; I'm sure she'll nip you. Why not mount and let Jill see how nicely you ride?'

'Oh, I can't be bothered,' said Ann. 'Let's go and look at the puppies instead.'

'Well, don't get your shoes muddy,' said Mrs Derry, 'and if you do, be sure to scrape them at the back door, and don't let the children handle the puppies – Ann! You've got a scratch on your hand. Oh, I hope it isn't going to turn septic like Pam's did –'

We got away at last and went to look at the West Highland puppies. I began to understand why Ann was not keen about riding or anything else.

However Mrs Derry was very kind and told me to go again whenever I liked, and I really felt that I had found a friend at last.

When I got home Mummy said I had better invite Ann to tea the following Saturday. I had a bright idea, and I told Ann to come on her pony so that we could do a bit of schooling together. She wasn't very keen, but at last she agreed to.

I was very excitedly waiting for her when she rode up on Seraphine. She looked very nice, in buff jodhpurs and a pepper-and-salt jacket, with proper jodhpur boots. I was in my grey denims, but Ann didn't appear to notice that I was not dressed like she was, which I appreciated.

Unfortunately when we got to the orchard Black Boy let me down! I hadn't had much time for him during the week, as I had been doing homework, and he was feeling high-spirited and defiant. So when he saw me coming with the halter – it was one that Martin had brought – he gave me a wicked look, flicked his heels, and made off. Our orchard ends in quite a large field, and here Black Boy had lots of space to tease me. I simply couldn't catch him, and I felt awfully silly in front of Ann.

She said, 'Let me try,' and she took the halter and walked towards Black Boy, speaking to him in a gentle but firm voice. And to my surprise, after one little sidling prance of defiance, he let her catch him and put on the halter.

This took me down a peg, for it showed that though she didn't even pretend to be keen, Black Boy recognized that Ann had experience and was not to be played about with.

I was waiting with the bridle, but the minute I took the halter off, before I could get the bridle on, Black Boy was off like the wind and stood still about twenty yards away, mischievously cropping grass and keeping one naughty eye on me to see what I'd do.

'I say,' said Ann, 'you really ought to put the reins over his neck before you take the halter off. Then you've got something to grab hold of if he tries to run out on you.'

'I know now,' I said. 'Actually Martin did tell me that, only I forgot. Now I've learned by bitter experience.'

So Ann had to catch Black Boy for me again, and this time all went well and we both mounted and rode out into the lane. I felt very nervous, as Ann took it for granted I could ride.

Although she said she didn't care about it she certainly rode very well, and understood all the aids and everything.

'I say, how do you make Seraphine take off on the right leg for cantering?' I asked. 'Black Boy takes off on the wrong one and it makes it so jolly uncomfortable.'

'Well, it's like this,' said Ann. 'Shorten your reins –
yes, that's right – and turn his head towards the left. Press

with both legs, but kick with your left foot. This will put
him off his balance, and he'll *have* to take off with his
offside leg to save himself. That's better – now you've got
it.'

'Oh, thanks most frightfully!' I cried, as Black Boy
responded with a perfect canter.

I could have gone on for ages, but Ann soon got
bored, so we went back home and turned the ponies into
the orchard, and then we went in and had tea over the
fire – Mummy had made hot buttered toast and marrow-
ginger – and I showed Ann my things and found she

liked the same books that I liked. What was more, she told me she had a lot of very good pony books at home which she would lend me.

'I've only got one ambition,' I said, 'and that's a terrific one – to ride in a gymkhana.'

'And I've only got one ambition,' said Ann, 'and that is *not* to ride in a gymkhana. Mummy made me enter for one last year and it was awful. I was nervous and forgot everything, and Seraphine knew I was nervous and played me up, and I was last in everything except the musical chairs, in which I was first out! So in a way I was last in that too. I felt the most awful fool, and Susan Pyke won three prizes and said to me afterwards, "Ann, you'll never do any good at a gymkhana until you learn to control your pony." I could have murdered her. Ever since then Mummy has been badgering me to enter for gymkhanas, and I won't. I won't – ever again!'

'You *could* ride as well as Susan Pyke,' I said, 'and you look a jolly sight nicer.'

'Oh, don't be feeble.'

'I'm not feeble. Oh, Ann, wouldn't it be simply super if one day you and I could enter for a gymkhana and take all the Firsts and Seconds, right under Susan's nose!'

'You are feeble!' said Ann witheringly, and I was afraid she was right.

# 7 - My little flock

ONE morning as I was biking to school I saw one of our small kindergarten kids standing with her mother at the gate of her home. The mother called to me, and I got off my bike.

'Oh,' she said, 'I was hoping an older girl would come along. You see, the young woman who takes Jennifer to school and brings her home is ill. Would you mind taking her with you, and collecting her again at twelve-thirty?'

So I took Jennifer, who was about five; and though it was a bit of a nuisance I collected her from the kindergarten at half past twelve and took her home. Then I rode my bike home the rest of the way.

The next morning the same thing happened again, except that there were two more small children, called Jane and Elizabeth, and their mother asked if I would take them too. So I did. And the next morning there was another one called Angela, so by now I had quite a flock. Apparently this girl who usually took them all had had to go to hospital and wouldn't be back for ages.

I felt I had got let in for something, only I just couldn't be mean to these small kids who seemed quite to like me, though Ann Derry shrieked with laughter when she saw me marching off, pushing my bike out of the school drive with these four infants trotting along behind me. The kindergarten only went to school in the mornings.

After I had been doing this for exactly a week I had a truly stunning surprise. Jennifer's mother handed me fifteen pence, saying that was what she gave the girl who usually took Jennifer, so of course I ought to have it. Then Angela arrived and handed me an envelope from her mother holding another fifteen pence, and on the way home we met the mother of Jane and Elizabeth who gave me twenty pence, because on two mornings I had had to wait for them to finish their music lessons.

I went home in a sort of daze. Fifty pence! And as the girl in hospital was said to be worse, next week I should have another fifty pence, and the week after that. . . .

I was so excited, and at the same time relieved. You see, for ages I had been worrying terribly about money, and how I was going to feed Black Boy in the winter, let alone stable him. And now – well, I might even collect a few more children; I might even make enough to cover all my expenses! So you can imagine why I was so happy and thrilled.

I went in whistling like mad and feeling the nice round solid feel of the silver in my blazer pocket; then I washed and went down to help Mummy make tea.

She said, 'You're very cock-a-hoop, Jill. Has something nice happened?'

I hadn't intended to tell her just then, but I couldn't keep it in, so I told her the whole story, and I said, 'Oh, Mummy, isn't it marvellous? I'll be able to buy everything for Black Boy now.'

But she looked rather serious, and after a moment she said quietly, 'Jill, you'll have to give all that money back at once.'

'What – what do you mean?' I said, feeling quite shaky with the shock.

'My dear, you can't accept it. You can't take money for

doing a simple act of kindness. Don't you understand?'

'Oh, Mummy!'

'You must give it back tomorrow morning, Jill.'

'But what shall I say?' I wailed.

'Say that your mother says you are to return the money, but you will be very glad to take the children to school as long as you are needed.'

'For nothing!'

'You didn't do it because you expected anything in the first case. Of course you may accept a sweet or an apple.'

'But –'

'That's enough. Now butter the toast and we'll have tea.'

After tea I went out and wept a bitter tear into Black Boy's mane, but I soon mopped it up and decided that I had better find some other way of making money.

I may add that I went on conducting those children all the term, and sometimes they asked me home to tea, and I had some very good teas and we talked about ponies, so it wasn't so bad after all.

But meanwhile I was faced with the problem of Black Boy and the approaching winter. I had simply got to stable him somewhere, and though I talked it over with Mummy we didn't seem to get any further, and of course it was really my responsibility after buying my pony so recklessly. But by now I loved him so much, and when I took him his daily carrot or apple he would talk to me with such lovely soft whiffley noises, that I felt the only thing that mattered in the world was finding him a home for the winter.

Of course I had not mentioned this worry of mine to Martin Lowe, because Mummy had said I must definitely not accept anything more from him, he was too generous already.

So one free afternoon I groomed Black Boy with the utmost care, spending ages on brushing out his mane and tail and cleaning his feet and making him shine all over; then I dressed in my clean white shirt and the grey denims out of which I had taken some marks with Thawpit, and I brushed my shoes and put on my school mac and hat, and I rode feeling very nervous to a nearby riding school – not the one that Susan Pyke went to, but another kept by a lady called Mrs Darcy.

When I got to the gate I saw that several ponies and horses were in the paddock, and a girl groom was crossing the yard carrying a bucket.

I said, 'Oh – good afternoon.'

'Have you come about lessons?' she said, looking at Black Boy unrecognizingly.

'Er – no,' I said. 'Please could I speak to Mrs Darcy?'

'Just a moment,' she said. 'I'll fetch Mrs Darcy.'

Mrs Darcy proved to be a lady with grey hair, wearing a khaki shirt and breeches and some very neat riding boots.

She looked at me, and said, 'Is it about riding lessons?'

'Well, no, it isn't – I'm afraid,' I said. 'It's just that – well, Mrs Darcy, I'm Jill Crewe and this is my pony Black Boy. I haven't anywhere to stable him for the winter, and I wondered if –'

'I'm afraid I don't stable ponies,' she said quite pleasantly; 'I haven't the accommodation.'

I felt myself going red.

'What I wondered was whether – whether you would care to use Black Boy in your riding school in return for stabling him,' I said, all in a rush.

'Oh.' She looked hard at Black Boy. 'Do you groom him yourself? He looks very nice.'

'Yes, I do.'

'Is he well schooled and trained?' she asked next.

'I – I'm really only just beginning to school him now,' I said.

She smiled kindly.

'I'm afraid he wouldn't be any use to me. You see, I can only use thoroughly well trained and schooled ponies who understand my teaching routine. And I couldn't offer an untrained pony even as a hack.'

'Yes, I see,' I said, my face falling.

I thought a moment and then said, 'Oh, Mrs Darcy, is there anything at all I could do, for Black Boy's stabling? I'd clean tack or do grooming or feeding or anything. I could come before school in the mornings, and at week-ends when you're busy.'

'I'm sorry,' she said. 'I have all the help I need.'

I knew then it wasn't any use, and I just said, 'Thank you,' and rode away.

## 8 - The stable

'Now we have got to get down to some serious school-ing,' said Martin. 'Our job is to mark out a riding school in that so-called field of yours. By the way, I wonder what happened to the hay from it?'

'Hay?' I said.

'Yes, hay. Somebody cut it and took it away before you came here, obviously. I'll bet it was Farmer Grimes, and that he's been doing it all the time the cottage was empty. There should be enough hay there to keep your pony supplied all winter. I'll see Grimes about it.'

'Hay!' I said again, looking quite pole-axed, because hay was one of the things I had had on my mind for ages.

'Haven't you ever heard of the stuff?' said Martin. 'You look as if you'd just had a load of it tipped over you. Now if you'll look on the floor of the chair, round my feet, you'll find, one – a tin of lime-wash, two – a brush, three – some pegs, four – yards and yards of twine. Do you know how to mark out a circle? Well, I'll tell you.'

Martin wheeled his chair into the middle of our field, and sat there while he instructed me how to measure out a wide ring with the pegs and mark it with the lime-wash. This took us till tea-time, when Mummy appeared in the orchard to call us. We went in as hungry as could be and even Martin who usually hadn't much appetite ate a huge tea. Then while I washed up and Mummy put the china away he told us funny stories until we were helpless with laughing.

Then we went to inspect the newly-made riding school.

I saddled Black Boy, and Martin made me ride round and round, walking, trotting, and cantering at his orders; and sometimes he would call me into the ring and make me turn and stand on the spot he told me to. I suppose I made rather a feeble show, because he made me do it over and over again.

'It isn't a case of will it do, Jill,' he said. 'It has got to be perfect.'

He then made me dismount and mount again several times. He was particularly fussy about dismounting, and reminded me that I must not swing off the pony or merely jump down, but do it the proper way; namely, to lift my right leg over and bring the foot close to the one in the stirrup; then to pause for an instant while I put my weight on my two hands; release the left foot from the stirrup and then spring from my hands to the ground. At last I was able to do this to satisfy him.

'Now spend a week in practising what I've shown you today,' he said, as it began to grow dusk.

'Thank you most awfully, I will,' I said; for I had realized by now that to be a good rider means endless patience and hard work, and it is no use thinking you have finished with the early stages and ought to go on to something more spectacular.

'You have forgotten something,' said Martin, as I dismounted and began to take off Black Boy's saddle.

'What?' I said.

'You've forgotten to pat your pony and thank him for what he has done. That's awfully important, Jill; you must never forget it. Whatever your horse does for you, always pat him, speak to him, and tell him he has done well. He understands, and your sympathy will help him next time. When you go to big shows and gymkhanas you will see how the best riders always pat and speak to their horses after – say – a jumping round.'

'Jumping?' I said. 'Oh gee!'

'Yes, jumping,' said Martin, 'and it isn't so far off from you as you think.'

I patted Black Boy and rubbed his cheeks, saying good night to him while I took off his bridle.

'Isn't it about time you put him in at nights?' said Martin casually.

My legs went all rocky.

'I – i – n?' I stammered.

'In the stable.'

'But – oh Martin, I can't find anybody who'll stable him, and Mummy said I wasn't to worry you about it and I haven't, have I? – but honestly I don't know what to do. I want a stable for Black Boy more than anything in the world.'

'Well, what's the matter with the one you've got?' said Martin.

'The – the what?'

'That!' said Martin, pointing at what we called the garden-shed which was really a rather tumbledown-looking building with a steep gable in which Mummy had stacked our trunks and boxes when we came to the cottage.

'Do you mean the shed?' I said. 'But –'

'Shed? It's a stable – at least it was when I used to come here and play with Tom Jarvis, years ago. Tom kept his pony there. Let's go and see, shall we?'

I didn't need inviting twice. I rushed to the shed and pulled out the padlock, releasing the hasp. The door opened, and revealed a medley of trunks and wooden boxes, piled up high.

I began to pull at the nearest, and when two or three had come out there was revealed a cobbled floor with a gutter running along it.

'Oh!' I yelled in my excitement.

I pulled away like mad at those boxes, and presently with a crash the whole lot descended; I fell flat on my back; Martin shouted, 'Look out!' and Mummy came running out of the house crying, 'What on earth has happened?'

'Mummy!' I shrieked, 'It's a stable! Look! I can see the manger. A proper stable. Oh gosh, I'm going mad.'

I jumped up and began to whizz round in circles, letting out whoops of joy.

'And what are you going to do with all my boxes?' said Mummy.

'Leave them to me,' said Martin. 'We've got loads of room at our place and I'll store them for you. Yes, there's a nice stall here for Black Boy, and a place for keeping tack and fodder too.'

'Thank goodness,' said Mummy. 'Now I shan't find corn and cleaning rags all over the kitchen.'

Martin ran his chair backwards a little way and peered upwards.

'In that gable there there's a small door, and I'm sure you'll find a useful hayloft there. It will do for your hay when I get it from Farmer Grimes.'

'What's this about hay?' said Mummy.

'Oh, Mummy, don't ask me questions yet!' I gasped. 'Such marvellous things are happening today I'm nearly crackers with joy.'

'You'll have a bit of work here,' said Martin. 'This

stable is filthy and you can't put Black Boy in yet. I'll tell you what, I'll send a man round to clean it out and give it a coat of whitewash –'

'Certainly not,' said Mummy. 'Jill can do everything herself, except for the whitewashing, and I'll help her with that. She is so thrilled about the stable that she will find the cleaning of it part of the fun.'

'But –' began Martin.

'Yes, I'd love to clean it out,' I said. 'It's all right. Mummy and I will do it in no time.'

'Do what?' said a voice, and I looked round to see Ann Derry standing there with her bicycle.

'Oh look, Ann,' I cried. 'We've found a stable that we didn't know we had. It's for Black Boy, and we're going to clean it out and whitewash it.'

'Goody,' said Ann. 'I'll come home with you after school on Monday afternoon, and help. Can I?'

'Rather!' I said.

Actually Ann turned out to be just as excited about cleaning out the stable as I was; and on Monday school seemed to drag terribly.

Directly we were released at four o'clock we flew back home and could hardly wait to eat the tea which Mummy had ready for us.

We got ourselves up in ghostly-looking overalls and tied dusters over our hair, and then we set to work.

It was fun. And soon the reason for Ann's excitement emerged. At home her mother would not allow her to do anything that was messy, but told the handyman to do it, or got a man in, whereas all sensible people know that really messy manual labour is one of the jolliest things in the world, when you are dressed for it and it doesn't matter how filthy you get.

We worked and worked until it got too dark to see properly, but still we went on, working by feel. We had taken it in turns to slap on the whitewash, which as you might say was the cream of the job in hand, and the inside of the stable looked splendid. We had swilled and brushed, and scrubbed the woodwork of the stall, and Ann had even brought some tile-polish for the cobbles! As they were originally grey, the red polish made them look as though somebody had spilled a sunset over them and the general effect was very chic.

At last it was all finished, and straightening our aching backs we went in for supper. Mummy melted down some cheese and Ann and I made hot toast, and we poured the cheese on the toast and added some grilled mushrooms which Mummy had found in the field that morning. (I don't mean they were grilled when she found them.) We had milky coffee to drink, and consumed this gorgeous meal sitting round the kitchen fire with our feet in the fender. I don't think even the queen had such a good supper that night.

A few days later – when Black Boy had begun to get used to his stable – along came a farm cart with a load of hay. It was just as Martin had thought; Farmer Grimes had cut the hay in June and taken it away, though in justice to him it must be said that the cottage had been empty for a long time and he hadn't known that we were coming or that we should keep a pony.

So he generously sent an awful lot of hay, quite enough for my pony for the whole winter, and the man who brought it very kindly forked it up into the loft above my stable (which Mummy and I had cleaned up in hopes).

Meanwhile Mummy took rather a dim view of all her trunks and boxes and things lying about the garden, until

Martin reminded her that they had loads of out-houses at his home where they should be stored and sent a cart to fetch them away. Of course this involved more gratitude and burdens of obligation towards Martin, but we really didn't see what we could do about it.

# 9 - Jumping

ONE day I had a letter which proved to be from Miss
Eileen Harvey, a friend of Martin's.

It said:

'Dear Jill,

'My mother and I are arranging a few days' riding
holiday at the half term and would be so pleased if you
would join our party. There will be about seven of us.
We are going to make our headquarters at a farm on the
Downs and go long rides each day, taking picnic lunches
and teas. Perhaps you would like to tell your mother
that the four days will cost under eight pounds for
yourself and your pony. I do hope you will be able to
come.

'Yours sincerely,
'Eileen Harvey.'

Well, actually I just put this letter in my pocket and
never told Mummy anything about it. It wasn't only the
eight pounds – though I wouldn't have thought of asking
Mummy for that sum since she hadn't had a holiday herself for ages – but it was the old, old question of not
having anything to wear. I couldn't go away for four
days with seven riding people in my grey denims, one
cotton shirt, and a school mac. So I wrote a letter to
Eileen Harvey saying that I was very sorry but I wouldn't
be able to get away at half term but it was frightfully
nice of her to have asked me. I hoped she wouldn't tell

Martin in case he thought that I hadn't wanted to go with his friends.

One day at school I said to Ann, 'I wish you'd come and bring Seraphine some Saturday afternoon. Martin wouldn't mind, and we could have a little gymkhana, just the two of us.'

At the hated word Ann's eyes goggled and she swallowed hard.

'All right then,' I said hastily. 'You needn't do a thing, but you can watch me and see if you can give me a hint or two. And do bring Seraphine, she would be such nice company for Black Boy.'

So in the end I persuaded her to come, and Martin gave her quite a welcome and the ponies seemed frightfully glad to see each other. I rode round the 'school', and after a bit I noticed that Ann was following me, which was a good sign. Before the afternoon was over she was getting quite interested.

Martin said, 'Do you jump, Ann?'

She said, 'Well, I did do, but I couldn't be bothered.'

'Jill is ready to begin jumping,' he said. 'It would be a tremendous help to her if you would do it with her. We'll have some easy jumps set up, and then you and Seraphine can take the lead.'

'Oh, do, Ann!' I cried. 'Oh, please do! I'm dying to jump, and I know I'll do it better if you're there to show me.'

'Oh, all right,' she said.

After that we set to work making jumps, and this being lovely messy work and manual labour of the hardest kind it appealed to Ann, just as cleaning the stable had done.

Martin got us a lot of wood, bars, hurdles, and nails,

and showed us how to fix them together. We constructed a triple bar with wings which looked marvellous until Ann accidentally leaned against it, when it fell apart and she sat down heavily on the ground.

We next made a gate of sorts, and also a box which we filled with heather. These things took ages to make and we had lots of fun over them. Ann said her father had bought her a set of jumps, and she hadn't realized that making them was a labour of such pleasantness.

All these jumps looked terrifically high to me, but they were actually about two-foot-six. Martin said that they must be made easy to knock down at a touch of the pony's foot, and ours were easy all right – too easy, as they usually fell down the minute the wind blew.

When the jumps were made, the next thing was to paint them, and the wings, white. We had a great time over this; Ann and I looked like snowmen when we had finished and there were dabs of white all over Martin's chair. I don't know how they got there! Mummy was concerned and said we must get turpentine and take them out, but Martin just laughed and said he looked upon them as worthy decorations.

The night before my first jumping lesson I couldn't go to sleep; and when at last I did I dreamed I was jumping twenty-foot walls with the greatest ease and Susan Pyke was watching me in speechless admiration.

When Martin arrived next day the first thing he did was to give Ann instructions to set up a pole across two bricks about a foot off the ground. This was to be my first jump.

'I feel weird,' I said.

'Nonsense,' said Martin. 'The jump is so low that you'll hardly notice it at all. The great thing to do is to grip with your knees and to keep your balance and go *with* the pony. Above all, you must *not* hang on to your reins to maintain your balance, or you will jag your pony's mouth and he will dislike jumping and refuse, quite rightly, to do it. Keep your legs still and firm, and slightly lean forward as you approach the jump, for he will swing back as you cross the obstacle and that has to be counteracted. Remember, *you* are not jumping; let the pony do the work, and I do *not* want to see daylight between you and the saddle, Jill. Now tighten your girths a little, and mount. Ann, take the lead and show Jill how easy it is.'

Ann walked, and then cantered easily up to the pole; in a split second and quite effortlessly Seraphine was over.

'Good!' cried Martin.

Now it was my turn. I put Black Boy at the jump and hoped for the best. I hardly felt him rise, and then realized that we were over!

'Jolly good!' said Martin. 'Easy, wasn't it? And Black Boy is going to love jumping. I can see it in his happy face. Do it again, two or three times, and then we'll raise the pole.'

To make a long story short, we jumped the pole several times, and also a low hurdle, and then Ann jumped by herself, a three foot jump, and looked quite pleased with herself.

'Oh, Ann!' I said. 'How beautifully you did it.'

'I quite enjoyed it,' she confessed. 'Riding here with you is much more fun than in the paddock at home with Mummy watching all the time and telling me how to do it.'

I felt as though I should never be tired of jumping, and on I went, over the low jumps, until to my surprise Black Boy presented me with my first refusal.

'It's no good, Jill,' said Martin laughing. 'He isn't having any more.'

'Why do horses refuse at jumps?' asked Ann. 'I've always wondered that at gymkhanas, because obviously the horse wouldn't be there if he wasn't a jumper.'

'Well, Ann, when a horse refuses at a jump the rider should first ask himself, is it *his* fault? Very often it is. The horse is not presented at the jump properly, or is held back too long or urged forward too late, or his stride is not quite right. The horse wants to jump well in most cases – though you will always see horses which are just being nappy on purpose. Even that may originally be the rider's fault. You must never, on any provocation, punish your horse for a refusal, however disappointed you may be. Give him another try; take him back calmly, pat him and speak encouragingly to him. Ten to one he will respond with every bit of his gallant nature and take you over the fence.'

'He could refuse because his tack was uncomfortable, couldn't he?' asked Ann.

'He certainly could. One of the most fidgety horses I ever saw in a show actually had a sore mouth from a too sharp bit. I can't tell you too often to take extra time and trouble to make sure that saddle, bridle, bit, and all tack is perfectly comfortable to your horse.'

'May I ask another question?' asked Ann.

'Ask fifty. That's what I'm here for.'

'Well, why do they have wings on jumps at all? Is it just to look well?'

'Or to make rocky jumps like ours stand up properly?' I said.

'Certainly not. The main use of wings is to make the horse go straight at the jump.'

'Oh yes, I see that,' said Ann. 'Thank you.'

'Now spend the week practising low jumps,' said Martin, 'and don't make that pony go on when he's sick of the game. You wouldn't like people to make you go on when you were sick of a thing. Next week I am going to test your balance by making you do the jumps with your arms folded before you. And later you will do the same with your stirrups up in front of the saddle.'

'Gosh!' I said. 'Circus tricks already. And last night I hadn't even jumped.'

'Not circus tricks at all,' said Martin calmly. 'Jumping is a matter of balance and gripping with the knees, as I said before. So if you can't do it without hanging on with toes and hands, then you aren't fit to jump at all.'

'Let's practise, Ann,' I said eagerly. 'Let's practise like mad and surprise him.'

'All right,' she said, unexpectedly. 'I'm game.'

# 10 - Christmas

I WOKE up on Christmas morning at peace with all the world. The day before Martin had set me a test of changing legs at the canter, getting my pony on the wrong leg and putting him back, and by good luck and with a bit of good management too I had done it perfectly and felt frightfully bucked.

He had praised my collected trot too, and that was something from Martin who never flattered and could be very sarky if you didn't appear to be trying, or showed impatience, or thought you knew everything.

It was still dark, and I lay there thinking how frightfully cosy it was and what marvellous institutions holidays were, when you didn't have to get up at practically midnight to muck out stables before going to school.

Then it occurred to me that after all it *was* Christmas morning, and something *might* have happened during the night, so I sat up in bed and lighted my candle – because our cottage hasn't got electric light and only gas downstairs – and sure enough there were several interesting things on the table beside my bed.

At first I thought I would wait until it was light, but I hadn't got the strength of character, so I picked up the first thing, which was a registered envelope from my godmother who lives at a place called Witten-le-Wold.

The envelope contained a pound note, and a card with a verse on it which said: 'The auld auld wish in the auld

66

auld way, frae a freend baith kind and true.' I wonder why
so many Christmas cards go all Scotch like this? I was
awfully pleased about the pound, which of course I
intended to spend on something for Black Boy.

The next thing I picked out was from Mummy, small
and narrow and wrapped in tissue paper tied with green
ribbon, and with a little tag tied on, saying, 'Merry
Christmas, darling.'

This parcel contained a fountain pen which I had
always wanted. However to show to what a depth my
squalid nature had descended, I admit that it promptly
occurred to me that the pen must have cost at least three
pounds, and could have been jodhpurs. But I put this
unworthy thought from me, because the pen was jolly
decent of Mummy.

I then inspected three quite interesting parcels, I mean
interesting from their shape. I do think the shape of
parcels tells you a lot. These three were from my cousin
Cecilia, who was then about fifteen, and my two aunts,
Olive and Dorothy.

Cecilia's parcel contained a book called *The Madcap of
the School*, and she had written in it, 'To Jill with best
Xmas wishes from Cecilia' and then for some unknown
reason, five x's. I must state that Cecilia had no intention
of being patronizing, as books like *The Madcap of the
School* are the ones she likes herself. (Mummy says it is
bad manners to write Xmas.)

Aunt Olive's parcel contained a card of a coach drawing
up outside an inn, and a manicure set of some little tools
with ivory handles; unfortunately people who muck out
stables and groom ponies have not the sort of hands that
manicure sets can do anything for.

Aunt Dorothy's card was of a bulldog dressed up in a

blouse and bell-bottomed trousers, and her present was a thin flat box of handkerchiefs with 'J' in the corner, which were quite useful only not very exciting.

There was still a parcel left, and I wondered if it could be from Martin. However it proved to be from Ann, and was a pair of jellow string gloves. I was quite overcome by this splendid present, which had a little card inside, quite plain except for 'Love from Ann' written on it; and then I was plunged into deepest gloom as I realized that I hadn't even thought of getting anything for Ann.

I couldn't stay in bed any longer, and a sickly dawn was now breaking, so I put my dressing-gown on and went into Mummy's room. She had lighted her candle too, and was sitting up in bed opening her presents. She said the one she liked best was the blue linen night-dress case I had made for her, with her initials worked on it.

I had a sudden thought and said, 'Stay where you are, Mummy, till I come back?'

Then I flew downstairs and put the kettle on the new gas-cooker we had got, and when it boiled I made her a cup of tea in the fluted green cup and saucer that she likes, and carried it up.

She said, 'Oh, what a treat! This is real luxury, tea in bed on Christmas morning.'

Then we got dressed and went down and had breakfast, and I took Black Boy an extra feed of oats for his present, and mucked out the stable.

When this whirl of toil was ended and we breathed again, I told Mummy about the lovely yellow string gloves and how awful it was not having sent anything to Ann.

'Oh, that's all right,' said Mummy. 'Ann brought the

parcel last night when you were in the stable, and I told her to come this afternoon and get her own present off our tree. Martin is coming too.'

'That was quite a brain wave,' I said, 'but we haven't anything to give her, have we?'

'Oh yes,' said Mummy. 'As a matter of fact I've got a spare copy of *Winnie Wish-Too-Much* and I'll autograph it. I'm sure Ann will like that.'

My lips said, 'Oh, that's marvellous,' but I gave a hollow inward groan. *Winnie Wish-Too-Much* was one of Mummy's least attractive efforts, about a girl who was always wanting things she hadn't got, until her fairy godmother sent her to live in the Town of Lost Happiness until she found the Key of Contentment. The way Winnie kept nearly finding the key and then just missing it made me, for one, feel seasick.

Anyway, Mummy autographed this book, and I wrote in it, 'Ann from Jill with love' and wrapped it in blue tissue paper and tied it on the little tree we always have at Christmas.

Then Mummy said it would be nice to go to church on Christmas Day and sing carols; so we did, and there were quite a lot of girls from school there, and afterwards we all said Hallo, and some of their mothers said Hallo to Mummy, which she liked as she didn't know many people in Chatton.

After dinner we cleared away and I washed up while Mummy wrote one or two thank-you letters, because if you don't do these in the first flush of enthusiasm you can't think what to say and even forget what the person sent you.

I had hardly finished when Ann arrived. To my surprise she was quite thrilled with the 'Winnie' book, and couldn't get over the fact that Mummy had written it. She said she would start reading it as soon as she got home and was sure she would love it as it would be a nice change from pony books.

About ten minutes later Martin arrived. First he handed me a parcel which contained a beautiful riding stick, just what I wanted, and then he handed Mummy a large bunch of purple grapes, the very luscious expensive kind that you usually have to be nearly dying to get.

Next I gave him my present off the tree, which was a rather nice and quite plain navy-blue tie, and he liked it very much, and Mummy gave him one of those calendars in a glass frame, where you take out cards and stick them in again and it goes on for ever.

'And now,' said Martin, 'for Black Boy's present. I thought he would rather have food than anything, so you will shortly be receiving enough corn to set him up for the rest of the winter. I hope it will be useful.'

I was so overcome that I stood there opening and shutting my mouth like a goldfish.

'What's up with you?' said Martin.

'Oh, Martin!' I gasped. 'You have taken such a frightful burden off my mind.'

But Mummy said at once, 'It's too much. We can't accept it, Martin. Feeding Black Boy is Jill's own responsibility and she must stand the expense. You give us too much and we can't repay you.'

Martin looked very serious.

'Repay?' he said slowly. 'There is only one thing that can't be repaid, and that is what I owe to you. You don't know what you and Jill have done for me, I don't think I'll ever make you understand. When I come here I feel I'm not only useful but happy. This is the only place where I forget – yes, actually forget – what's wrong with me.'

'Oh, but you must have so many friends,' said Mummy, while I stood wondering.

'Yes, many friends. But – oh, can't you understand –

when I'm with them it's awful. They knew me as I used to be. They try and adapt themselves to me as I am now. They try not to say or do anything that would make me realize what I've missed. And all the time I can see in their eyes, "Poor old Martin, how rotten for him." Perhaps it's because you and Jill didn't know me before. Whatever it is, this is the one place I look forward to coming to, the place where I have fun. And you talk of owing me anything. It's I who owe you everything.'

After making this long speech Martin went red and looked very awkward, and I was tongue-tied too, but Mummy rose to the occasion and said, 'Thanks, Martin, that's very nice of you and I understand. We won't talk about obligations any more; we'll just say thank you.'

After that we all had tea, and everything looked rosy to me, and we had iced buns and a proper Christmas cake that an old friend of Mummy's had made and sent to her. But the delights of this day were not over. While we were having tea there was a knock at the door, and when I went to answer it a boy handed me a very large soft parcel, saying, 'This is for Miss Jill Crewe.'

'Gosh! Thanks!' I said, and carried it in.

'It's for me,' I said, holding it out to let Mummy see. 'Is this something to do with you, Martin?'

'No,' he said. 'Cross my heart, I know nothing about it.'

'Who on earth can it be from?' I said.

'Do open it and see,' said Mummy.

The magnificent thing was soon revealed, a lovely dark-blue pony rug bound round with scarlet. I was speechless. It was Mummy who picked up the card and read aloud, 'To Jill Crewe, with many thanks, from the mothers of Jennifer, Angela, Jane and Elizabeth.'

'I don't know how they knew,' I said. 'Honestly I didn't say anything to them, Mummy. I can't guess how they knew.'

(Afterwards I found out that they had asked Ann what I would like and she had suggested the rug.)

Of course the first thing I did was to rush off to try the rug on Black Boy. He looked wonderful with it on, and exactly like a blood pony, and he arched his neck and bucked a bit, just showing off because he knew how nice he looked; so I walked him up and down in front of the cottage windows and Mummy and Ann and Martin waved approval.

After getting all these wonderful presents, especially the horsy ones that I hadn't expected, I think you will agree with me that it was a very nice Christmas.

# 11 - Cecilia's visit

A FEW days later I took Black Boy to the forge, and while Mr Blankett the smith was engaged in shoeing him he happened to say, 'If you haven't got a double bridle, miss, I've got a nice one here for sale. It belongs to a gentleman who's going abroad and selling off all his used tack before he goes. I'll fetch it in a minute.'

So when he had finished Black Boy he went and fetched the bridle which really was a very nice one, and though well used had been well cared for, with the leather supple and clean and the bits and curb chain shining.

I said, 'I expect it's rather expensive.'

'Oh, no,' said Mr Blankett. 'He wants to get the stuff sold. He's asking a pound for this, but I think he'd take eighty pence.'

So of course I just dived into my pocket for my god-mother's pound note, and having got twenty pence change which went towards the shoeing I thought I had done very well indeed. I felt that my stable was getting well equipped; and it was such a thrilling thought after my weeks of making do and using makeshifts, that on the way back I let Black Boy buck and prance and do all the things he shouldn't do, just for sheer joy.

It was a lovely winter day, with a pale blue sky and sunlight brightening the red berries in the hedgerows and making the puddles glitter along the road.

When I got home the post had arrived, and Mummy

said, 'There's a letter from Cecilia's mother. She has to go to Ireland next week on business and she wonders whether Cecilia could come here for a few days. Of course we'll be glad to have her, won't we, Jill?'

'O.K.' I said.

'I'll write out a telegram and you can bike down to the post office and send it at once. And, Jill, you'll have to sleep with me and let Cecilia have your room.'

'Oh blow!' I said. But I knew this would have to be as we only have two bedrooms at the cottage.

'Of course,' said Mummy, 'if you'd rather sleep with Cecilia in my room and let me go in yours –'

'Oh no, she can have my room,' I said, but I began to feel very unenthusiastic about Cecilia's visit. I don't know how it is, but having to give up your room to a guest always seems to arouse murderous feelings in the breast.

The following week, on the Tuesday, Mummy and I went down to Chatton to meet Cecilia's train. I was actually feeling more than a bit scared, as fifteen is just on the verge of being grown up and I didn't know how Cecilia would react to me being not quite twelve. However when she got off the train I saw that she wasn't any taller than I and didn't look at all grown up, not so much so as our prefects at The Pines School. She had plaits, and was wearing a brown school mac and a school hat right at the back of her head.

'Hallo, Aunt Catherine!' she said. 'Hallo, Jill!' And she kissed us both in a very friendly way, which struck me, as I am not very good at kissing myself.

On the way home in the bus Cecilia said, 'And what are you doing with yourself these days, Jill?'

I said, 'Well, actually, I'm learning to ride.'

'What, still?' she said. 'I thought you learnt weeks and weeks ago.'

'I'm only just beginning,' I said.

'Good gracious!' said Cecilia. 'It's not so difficult, surely. Isn't it just a matter of learning to hang on?'

I shuddered slightly, and said, 'As a matter of fact, you can spend a lifetime learning to ride. If you are a really good horseman you know there's always something new to learn.'

'Good gracious!' said Cecilia.

However when we got home she went into ecstasies over the cottage and said that the garden reminded her of that 'God Wot' poem and she would send Mummy a copy to hang up; and then I took her to my bedroom and she said she had always wanted to sleep in a bedroom with a sloping roof and she thought it was all simply wizard.

She then went to my bookshelf to look at my books and I knew she would be looking for the one she had sent me for Christmas so I had put it rather towards the middle.

Cecilia said, 'Oh, there's the one I sent you, *The Madcap of the School*. Didn't you love it? I've got all Sallie T. Scott's books and I've read them over and over again until I nearly know them off by heart. There's *A Fourth Form Secret,* and *Prefect Patsy*, and *Sonia's First Term*. Don't you adore school stories? I never read anything else.'

'As a matter of fact,' I said, 'I get enough school in term time not to want to read about it in the hols, but,' I added, so as not to look disobliging, 'I know a lot of people read those books and I expect they're frightfully good if you're keen on that kind of thing.'

Cecilia looked at the rest of my books in a rather bleak

sort of way; and then I said, 'Shall we go down and see my pony before tea?' and she said she'd like to.

So we went down to the orchard and I called Black Boy and for once he came. Cecilia patted his nose, and said, 'You don't hunt, or anything, do you?'

I looked a bit blank, and said, no I didn't hunt or anything.

Cecilia said, 'Where do you ride?' so I showed her my riding school in the field, and then I saddled and bridled Black Boy and rode him round the ring a few times and he behaved beautifully.

'Good gracious!' said Cecilia. 'Is that all you do? I mean, just sitting on the pony and holding it in?'

'What I was doing,' I said, 'was a collected trot. I'll show you a collected canter, if you like, and a figure of eight with Black Boy changing legs in the middle, only I'm not frightfully certain of it yet.'

'Don't you ever do proper riding?' said Cecilia.

I felt myself boiling inside, and thought now I should have swooned with shame if Martin had heard this remark. I had been going to invite Ann to tea on Saturday, but thought I had better not. It looked as though Cecilia was going to turn out to be the stain on the family escutcheon, as it says in books.

The next day Cecilia looked on with horror while I mucked out and fed Black Boy, but she thought it was fun to put down fresh straw, and she got quite enthusiastic over the hens and thought them 'sweet'. As it happened Mummy had a cold, so I had offered to do the hens for once. It looked as though Cecilia was a henny rather than a horsy person. She said, wasn't it cruel to take their eggs away from them? And when I replied that all hens thought about was food and they were incapable

of any sublimer feelings, I could tell she thought I was a
callous and hardbitten woman.

She looked very disapproving when I said, 'Get off it!'
to Maria Marten, who was a dopey type of fowl, and gave
her a push out of the box.

When we went in to breakfast Cecilia said she didn't
like porridge and could she have some cornflakes? We
hadn't got any cornflakes, so she said she would just have
a lightly boiled egg. Mummy said that after breakfast I
had better go down to Chatton on my bike and get some
cornflakes for Cecilia, which I did. Cecilia said she didn't
want to come, as she always read after breakfast in the
holidays.

When I got back with the wretched cornflakes I found
that Mummy had washed up and made the beds, while
Cecilia was still reading. Then she said she would like to
write to her mother, which took her about an hour, and I
showed her where the box was in the lane to post her
letter, but that didn't suit her at all, as she said that somebody she knew had once posted a letter in a box in a
country lane and it hadn't got to where it was going for
about a week, so she wanted her letter to be posted at a
proper post office.

Mummy said I had better get my bike out again and go
back to Chatton and post Cecilia's letter, so I did this, and
so the dreary morning was spent.

The next morning at breakfast Mummy put out the
cornflakes for which I had made my toilsome journey, but
Cecilia only took one mouthful and then put her spoon
down with a kind of patient-under-suffering look.

'Is there anything the matter with the cornflakes?'
asked Mummy.

'Oh no, Aunt Catherine,' said Cecilia. 'They're most

awfully nice really, only they're just not a bit like the ones I have at home, so if you don't mind I'll just have a lightly boiled egg.'

As you know, January is not what you'd call a lavish month for eggs, so Cecilia was pretty well appropriating our whole production.

I said I simply must give Black Boy some exercise today, so we went out. Cecilia rode my bike, and we went as far as Neshbury Common. Cecilia didn't think anything at all of my riding and she didn't think I would ever make a rider until I let myself go and wasn't afraid to give my pony his head. She said that a lot of her friends were marvellous riders, and their ponies were full of spirit and showed it and they galloped about and looked simply terrific.

I thought I would show Cecilia the kind of thing she evidently liked, so I sat well back in the saddle and thumped Black Boy with my heels, and he must have thought I had gone mad. However he rose to the occasion and bucked and side-stepped, and then went off at a mad uncontrolled pace and threw his head about, and I bounced up and down in the saddle, and when we got back Cecilia clapped her hands and said, 'Oh, jolly good! That was marvellous. You see, you can ride after all when you try.'

I was mopping my brow with relief at having got through that fearsome exhibition without being seen by anybody who knew me.

'Could I have a try?' said Cecilia.

'Well, actually, Black Boy's had enough for today,' I said doubtfully.

'Oh, you are mean,' she said.

So I had to say all right. Getting Cecilia into the saddle

was like getting a sack of potatoes on to a lorry, but at last she was up. She stuck her feet straight out in front of her, leaned well back, pulled at the reins with a sprightly jerk, and said, 'Come up, now. Come up!'

It was too much for Black Boy. For the first and only time in his life he actually reared and stood straight up

on his hind legs. Cecilia gave a scream and slid off, making a wild grab at his tail and fortunately missing it. She sat down with a thud on the grass, and to my relief Black Boy promptly came back to earth, and with a look at me, as much as to say, 'No more of this, if you please,' stood still in offended dignity.

'Oh!' said Cecilia. 'What an ill-bred horse! No well-bred horse *ever* rears. A man who knows all about horses told me that. You'll have to get rid of him. He's what they call a confirmed rearer.'

'He's nothing of the kind,' I said. 'He's never done it

before and he'll never do it again. He's not used to having his mouth jerked like that.'

'Well, what on earth are the reins for?' said Cecilia getting up and brushing bits off her skirt, and smiling the slow superior smile of one who knows.

After this I started counting the hours to Cecilia's depature. I had to endure one final insult, when on the morning before she left she said innocently, 'Do you always ride in a mac and jeans? Shouldn't you have breeches and a jacket and bowler, or don't they bother round here?'

I honestly don't think she meant this maliciously, but I had my arms full of hay at the moment, and I could easily have smothered her with it.

However the darkest hour of human suffering comes to an end (Mummy's library book) and at last we were standing on Chatton station waving good-bye as Cecilia's train disappeared into the tunnel.

Mummy said, 'I don't think you liked Cecilia very much, did you, dear?'

'I thought she was awful,' I said frankly.

'You mean, she didn't like the same things that you liked. As grown-ups say, she didn't speak your language. But, Jill, you mustn't be intolerant. You must make allowances for the other person's point of view, and look for a common ground of interest instead of emphasizing your differences. It's the only way to live happily in a world where there are so many, many kinds of people.'

'Did you like her, Mummy?' I asked.

'Yes, I did. She has charming manners and listens to what her elders have to say without interrupting.'

I gave a contented sigh. Cecilia was gone, so it wasn't worth starting an argument with Mummy.

# 12 - Jodhpurs

I COULD now clear three-foot jumps easily, and wished I had something better to practise on than my queer home-made affairs.

It was a great piece of luck for me that Black Boy liked jumping and was never reluctant to try, but all the same Martin said that I must learn the proper way to aid a pony who *was* nervous or reluctant. So he invited me to go over to his home, The Grange, one Saturday in March and try a pony he had there.

I was very bucked at the invitation but more than a bit scared also. The night before, I scrubbed my mac with Mummy's nail brush and took all the spots off my jeans, and I washed and ironed my socks, shirt and tie, and brushed my hat and shoes.

I set my alarm for 6.30 next morning so that I should have lots of time to give Black Boy a special grooming. I crept downstairs in the chilly dawn, lit the fire, and put a kettle on the gas ring. Then I fed and groomed my pony, keeping one eye on the kettle because I know what kettles are if you don't do this.

When it boiled I climbed on a chair and got Mummy's soap-flakes out of the corner cupboard where she thinks she has hidden them, and made a lovely lather and washed Black Boy's tail, and while it was drying I crawled about the kitchen floor, taking up the tell-tale bits of soap-flake with my handkerchief. I suppose you think this was very wicked of me, but I am surprised if you haven't done such deeds yourself, and everyone knows that the best quality soap-flakes are the nicest thing for washing a horse's tail.

Then I brought all the tack into the kitchen and cleaned it in front of the fire. I worked like a Trojan for about two hours altogether, and by then I was so ravenous that breakfast tasted specially good.

After breakfast I did my room and then began to dress. I stood in front of the mirror, wondering how I could make myself look more than twelve. In the end I combed my hair well and fastened it behind my ears with some of Mummy's grips.

'Oh gosh!' I thought. 'If only I had a hard hat I should look about fifteen.'

But this was a vain hope. However, even with my school hat on, the new hair style made me look quite a bit sophisticated, though I didn't look in the least how I wanted to look which was like a girl who worked in a stable.

When I got to The Grange, Martin's father saw me and came out and shook hands with me in a very grown-up way. He said he had heard a lot about me from Martin, and I didn't know what to say because you never do when anybody says that kind of thing to you, so I just sort of smirked and said, 'Oh.'

Then he took me inside and introduced me to Martin's mother, who was rather old-fashioned and grand-mother-ish and was sitting in an easy chair reading *The Times*.

I tried to look nonchalant and horsy, as I could tell this had been a horsy household from all the photographs and cups and horse brasses and whips that were hanging on the walls and strewn about, but it was rather spoilt when Mr Lowe said, 'This is the little girl that Martin is teaching to ride.'

And Mrs Lowe said, 'And what did you say your name was, my pet?'

So I just said, 'How do you do? I'm Jill Crewe,' and I pushed in one of the grips, drawing attention to my sophisticated hair-style.

Just then Martin came bowling in in his chair, and said, 'Hurrah, you've come. Now we'll cut the cackle and get to the 'osses.'

We went right through the house and out at the back, and it all looked like a most beautiful dream to me when I saw the long, low stable buildings and horses' heads looking over half-doors. The Lowes, unlike other people who had pulled down their stables or converted them into garages and flats for their friends, could not bear to live without horses, and Mr Lowe – who had won heaps of driving and hackney classes in his time – still kept a high-stepping hackney for his own use, and Mrs Lowe had a pair of matched greys and went to visit her friends in a carriage in the old-fashioned way. Mr Lowe was fond of buying and selling horses too, and so the stables at The Grange were always happily filled. I thought it must be a heavenly place to live.

There was a nice smiling groom there who led out a roan pony of about fourteen hands for me to try.

'This is Silvio,' said Martin. 'It will be very good for you to ride him, because you will find that he does not read your mind and anticipate your wants like Black Boy does, and he will wait for direction from you.'

It was funny to see the look on Black Boy's face when he saw me mount Silvio. It was fun riding Silvio, but I had to be on my mettle because he didn't do a thing except when I gave him the right aid. I felt I was making a mess of it, but Martin actually said, 'Jolly good.' This didn't elate me as it would have done six months before, because by now I had learned the true humility of a rider.

Then two boys came out and erected three jumps for me to try. I was so used to Black Boy's enthusiasm at the very sight of jumps, that I felt queer when I noticed that Silvio sort of sneered in a distasteful way, as much as to say, 'Oh bother! Jumping again.'

Therefore I was prepared when he refused the first jump, a rare experience for me. I patted him and spoke to him, took him back and put him at it again, but again he refused. So I tried all over again, and all I got was a third refusal.

'Oh gosh!' I said to Martin.

He roared with laughter.

'It's up to you, Jill,' he said.

I took Silvio back, and whispered in his ear, 'Oh, Silvio, dear Silvio, for heaven's sake jump it or you'll cover me with disgrace for ever.'

We tried again, and this time he made a very bored effort and down came the whole gate.

'Oh help!' I said, looking back disgustedly.

'Jill,' said Martin, 'I warned you to expect no assistance from that horse.'

'No assistance!' I said. 'That's putting it mildly.'

'If you want to know,' said Martin, 'Silvio's stride was not right for the jump – which you ought to have seen to – and you said "Hup" just about one-twentieth of a second too soon.'

'If he's going to be as fussy as that about details –' I began.

'He's a born obeyer, is Silvio. He likes to obey, and he puts the whole of the burden of *thinking* on to his rider. Now try jumping the bush. He is used to being held in until the exact second when he must go right for the jump. It is for you to learn what is that exact second and give him his aids. Off you go!'

By now I didn't expect much from Silvio, but I tried frightfully hard and soon I did begin to get better results. Before the morning was over I felt that I really had learned something about jumping. Then, because Black Boy had been watching Silvio enviously for so long, I changed on to my own pony and put him over the jumps twice and it seemed so easy and effortless that I fairly sighed with relief.

But I quite realized that I could never call myself a horsewoman until I could cope with horses like Silvio, and far, far worse.

I thanked Martin very much for giving me the chance, and he said, 'That's all right. I hope you'll come again often, in fact you'll have to before the gymkhana season begins.'

'Why? What has that to do with me?' I said.

His eyes widened.

'I hope you're going to do me credit,' he said. 'Surely you want to ride in gymkhanas?'

'*Want to!*' I cried. 'I can't imagine anything more marvellous. But I never thought I'd be able to for years and years. I'm not nearly good enough. I'll make an awful fool of myself.'

'I shouldn't enter you if I thought that,' said Martin.

'To ride in a gymkhana!' I said. 'Oh crumbs!'

'Don't look so awed,' he said, laughing.

'But it's the dream of my life. I mean, to ride round the ring with a rosette at my pony's ear and a certificate in my teeth.'

'Is that why you want to enter for a gymkhana?' said

Martin. 'If I thought it was I wouldn't be so keen on entering you.'

'Why?' I said. 'Don't you want me to win?'

'Of course I do. But I say that the type of rider who enters a gymkhana simply with the idea of winning cups and rosettes has no business to be there at all. I should hate you to be that kind of person, Jill, but I'm quite sure that you won't be. What do you suppose gymkhanas are for?'

'I suppose, to give people a chance to show that they can ride and compete with others,' I said.

'Partly,' said Martin. 'But the real purpose of any gymkhana is simply to raise the standard of horsemanship and to bring out the best in horses and riders. Remember that. And now we'll go in and have some coffee and cakes.'

So we went indoors and had lovely elevenses – only it was twelve o'clock by then – and Mrs Lowe told me about her greys and how long she had had them, and I listened very intelligently and I'm sure she thought I was about fifteen.

All the way home I was singing, 'Gymkhana! Gymkhana! Gymkhana!'

As usual Mummy had a few things to say about my having gone mad.

It was a few days after this that one afternoon she gave me one pound fifty to call for my shoes which had been soled and heeled; so after school I set out for the cobbler's shop which is in the main street at Chatton, and in case anyone is interested, his name is Mr Price and he does the shoes really well with leather that lasts and not brown paper.

On the way I passed the auctioneer's place, and the doors were open and a crowd of people inside. I couldn't resist stopping to listen, though it turned out he was selling frightfully dull things like sets of wine-glasses and skin rugs.

I wormed my way through the crowd, right up to the edge of the table where the various rather scruffy-looking lots were set out, and all of a sudden my eye fell upon something that looked cordy and fawn-coloured. I thought at first it must be a bit of a skin rug, but with my usual curiosity I pushed my way up to this object and poked it open with my fingers.

Then my jaws fell apart and I'm sure my eyes stood right out. 'It' was a rolled up parcel consisting of a pair of jodhpurs and a little check jacket, and at a glance I could see that they would just fit me.

I simply couldn't believe it; it was like a fairy tale. When I came more or less to my senses I noticed that the jodhpurs had a ticket on with Lot 233 printed on it in red.

The auctioneer was just shouting out, 'Lot 225,' which was a marble clock with brass angels on the top. The next few minutes went by in a kind of daze; I wanted those jodhpurs and that jacket so terribly, and I knew that in a minute they were going to be auctioned and I should see them knocked down to some awful undeserving person and I couldn't bear it.

How much would they fetch? Probably pounds and pounds. That marble clock had just been sold for the fabulous sum of five pounds sixty-two and a half.

I looked at Mummy's money in my hand, which was to pay for my shoes being soled and heeled and leave some change over.

'Lot 233,' said the auctioneer. 'Pair of girl's jodhpurs and riding jacket. Now here's a lovely lot, one of the finest lots I've had through my hands for many a long day. Buy this fine outfit for your daughter and there's nothing to stop her being England's premier lady jockey. See her win the Grand National. Now, ladies and gentlemen, what am I bid for this really magnificent outfit of the finest quality. Somebody give me a start, please.'

There was silence. My heart turned over. Actually I might have known that in a place like Chatton people who bought riding outfits didn't have to buy them secondhand, and that this was a set that some child had outgrown and there wouldn't be much demand for it.

'Give me a start, ladies and gentlemen, *please!*' said the auctioneer in a very pained voice.

'Twenty-five pence,' said a voice at the back, fairly reluctantly.

The auctioneer looked round in patient suffering.

'Very well, very well. We'll start at twenty-five, though that is simply a joke for this fine riding outfit which is worth ten pounds of anybody's money. Twenty-five I'm offered, twenty-five pence I'm bid. Now ... forty. Forty, *please!*'

There was quite a silence.

I gave a little gasp, and the next minute the auctioneer had looked at me and said, 'Thank you, madam. I'm bid forty by the young lady. Now fifty pence ... fifty pence, please.'

This time the silence was awfully long. My excitement was crawling all up me and getting into my throat. At last the man at the back must have given a nod because the auctioneer, looked straight at me and said, 'Now, madam, there's fifty pence bid against you. Make it sixty-two and a half? Sixty-two and a half for this magnificent riding outfit which I can see will just fit you. Sixty-two and a half, madam, *please.*'

'All right,' I said with a dry throat.

'Any advance on sixty-two and a half?' said the auctioneer, looking round, but nobody said anything, and the next minute his hammer came down with a crack.

'Sold to the young lady in the school hat. Next Lot 234.'

Still I couldn't believe it. I pushed my way up to a man who was writing in a book and said, 'Please can I pay and take my things away?'

'Certainly, madam,' he said, very politely, and he looked at his book and said, 'Sixty-two and a half, please,' and I gave him a pound note – Mummy's – and he gave me thirty-seven and a half, and a receipted bill, and I went up to the table and took beautiful Lot 233 in my arms and walked out into the street with it, feeling all shot up and weak.

I had just enough mind left to go and collect my shoes and pay the eighty-seven and a half for them, and I biked home wondering what Mummy would say. Of course I knew I had no business to spend her money on things for myself, but somehow it all seemed to have been meant, as though the fairies had done it. Surely Mummy would see this.

Still money was money, and I did know very well that Mummy was going through a tough time. There hadn't been any cheques for a long time, and Mummy simply never bought anything for herself. She hadn't had anything new to wear for longer than I could remember, and I had had all that new school uniform. She had been what she called 'budgeting for every new penny' and here was I gaily flinging more than half of a pound note into the maw of an auctioneer in return for jodhpurs.

Oh, but I hugged my parcel. It was just a dream come true.

I took my bike round to the back of the cottage, and walked into the kitchen with my parcel in my arms, and stood wondering what to say.

'Hullo, Jill,' said Mummy. 'You're a bit late, aren't you? Did you go to Ann's? Oh, of course, you had to fetch your shoes. How much were they?'

Then she looked at me, and said, 'What have you got there?'

'Oh, Mummy,' I said, all in a burst. 'It's jodhpurs. Look. I – I –' and out came the whole story, though it was a bit jumbled up, what with excitement and guilty conscience.

'Oh,' said Mummy when I'd finished, and looked a bit blank. Then she said, 'You know you shouldn't spend money on yourself that I'd given you for something else.'

'Yes, I know,' I mumbled, going very red, 'but – but I'd been simply dreaming about jodhpurs for ages and ages, and it – it seemed like magic.'

Mummy sighed.

'I know,' she said. 'I – I ought to have guessed. It's all right, Jill, only don't buy anything else without asking me, will you? I mean, money is money.'

I rushed at her and enveloped her in a bear hug.

'Oh, thank you, Mummy!' I said in a heart-felt way. 'And I won't do it again because I know I' oughtn't to, with no cheques, and you never having anything yourself, and I do feel a pig about it honestly, only just to *see* them lying there –'

'That horse!' said Mummy. 'I knew what it would be.'

'Oh golly!' I said. 'I must go and feed him.'

'And as for these things,' said Mummy looking with

strange distaste at my beautiful jodhpurs, 'goodness knows where they've come from.'

'Oh that doesn't worry me,' I said. 'Only nice people have jodhpurs, anyway.'

'I'm not so sure,' said Mummy. 'Anyway, they're dirty and so is the jacket, and I suppose you've noticed – but of course you wouldn't – that one elbow is out and there are three moth holes in the collar –'

'Oh that's nothing,' I said hastily.

'Well, you must take them to the cleaner's. You'd better do it tomorrow, and that'll be about *another* fifty pence!'

This thought made me feel awful and just put the lid on all my pleasure. I couldn't even tell Mummy to take the fifty pence out of my pocket money because I actually owed her quite a bit already that I'd had in advance the week before.

I was plunged into blackest gloom as I went out to the orchard to catch Black Boy, and when he didn't come at once I spoke to him crossly, which I think was the first time I had ever done so, so it shows how my nature was becoming depraved.

I felt more awful still when next morning I found that Mummy had done the things up in a nice neat parcel for me to take to the cleaner's; but I didn't say anything, and took them on my way to school, and the woman gave me two tickets. One said Jodhpurs 25p and the other said Jacket 25p.

A week later Mummy gave me the fifty pence and I went to collect the things. When I opened them out in the kitchen they looked so nice that I had to give a gulp, and just then Mummy came in and said, in an understanding way, 'Don't look so blue, Jill. We're not ruined yet.'

## 13 - The bring and buy sale

It was amazing how my riding improved after I got my jodhpurs. I began to feel I was really getting on and could nearly call myself a rider, though Mummy said this feeling was psychological.

Funnily enough, I don't think Martin even noticed my lovely new rig-out, and if he did he didn't say a word about it, but Mummy said that men are like that.

When I went round to Ann's on the Saturday afternoon, she said at once, 'Gee whizz! You do look smashing.'

I said, 'Let's go for a ride somewhere,' and for once she was quite enthusiastic.

One day during eleven o'clock break at school, Ann said to me, 'What are you grunting and sighing about?'

'I was just thinking,' I said.

'What about? That awful Latin?'

'No. I say, Ann, you don't by any chance know any ways of raising money, do you?'

'Of course,' she said surprisingly. 'It's easy.'

'*Easy!* What on earth do you mean?'

'It's easy,' she repeated. 'Mummy's always raising money. You just have a Bring and Buy Sale. They had one last week at Mrs Fairedge's and raised about forty pounds.'

'Forty pounds!' I gasped. 'Easy! What on earth's a Bring and Buy Sale? How do you do it?'

'Well, you have it at somebody's house,' said Ann.

'You have a table in the garden, or in the dining-room if it's wet, and you stand behind the table and say, "Hallo, Mrs Derry. Frightfully nice of you to come along," and heaps of people come, and they all bring something to sell and put it on the table, and then they all buy something and go home. And at the end you have heaps of money.'

'But doesn't it cost you anything?' I asked.

'Of course not, silly. People bring something and then they buy something and go away. It sort of balances out, and you get the money.'

'I never heard of it,' I said, overwhelmed by the brilliance of this simple scheme. 'It sounds terrific. I say, Ann, do you think you and I could have one?'

'A what?'

'A Bring and Buy Sale, or whatever you call it.'

She gave a whoop.

'Oh, I say, what fun! Oh yes, Jill, let's. Do you mean at your house? When?'

I began to think furiously. I wanted to do this Bring and Buy Sale thing all by myself, and I thought it would be as well to have it when Mummy wasn't there as she might fuss and worry about having things just right. As it happened, she had talked about going to see an old school friend of hers the following Saturday; and as this old friend lived about twenty miles away, it would mean that Mummy would have to leave our cottage about ten o'clock to catch the bus in Chatton, and she couldn't possibly be back before about six, so that would leave us heaps of time for a Bring and Buy Sale. What a thrill it would be when she came back if I could tell her, quite casually, that I had raised forty pounds very, very easily! It *must* be all right to have a Bring and Buy Sale if Ann's mother did it, because Mrs Derry was such a very particular person.

So I said to Ann, 'Look here. Mummy's going away for the day on Saturday. Let's have the Bring and Buy Sale then, in our garden. It will be fun. You know all about it, so you can come round early and help me with the arranging.'

Ann was jumping about with excitement by now, and I was pretty well topped-up myself. We could hardly wait for Saturday to come, and then my heart sank into my shoes on Friday night when Mummy said, 'If it's a wet day tomorrow I shan't go.'

So about five o'clock on Saturday morning I was leaping out of bed and rushing to the window to see what sort of a day it was going to be. Everything looked dry and sort of hopeful, even at that early hour which is usually so depressing, and it turned out to be a lovely, bright, sunshiny spring day.

Of course Mummy fussed a lot about leaving me alone, even when I told her that Ann was coming to spend the day with me. I nearly told her about the Bring and Buy Sale, only I didn't want to raise her hopes until I actually knew how much money we had got.

At last she was ready, and I went with her to the bus stop and saw her on to the bus, and waved until she was out of sight. Then I went back to the cottage, and it had that funny silent feeling that houses have when you are in them alone. I can never understand this, because even if there is a person in another room where you can't see them, you don't get that funny hushed feeling.

However about five minutes later Ann arrived, and we started writing notices on sheets of paper torn out of our map books, which are rather large, using red crayon to write with.

BRING AND BUY SALE

AT

POOL COTTAGE, POOL LANE
THIS AFTERNOON AT 2 UNTIL ABOUT 4.30

We thought we had better stop about 4.30 so as to clear up and have our tea before Mummy got back, only if business was brisk we could always go on a bit longer.

We fastened one of the notices on our garden gate with drawing pins, because actually a lot of people go along Pool Lane, and then we biked to the end of the lane where it joins Greenwood Road, and we fastened another notice to the hedge there with safety pins.

Then we went back home and began to make our preparations. Actually it didn't take long, as all we had to do was to carry out the kitchen table and put it inside the little garden shed, after we had taken the garden tools out to make more room. It looked a bit bare, so I brought down the Paisley shawl off Mummy's bed and we covered the table with it.

Then we wrote another notice which said, THIS WAY TO THE BRING AND BUY SALE, and then a lovely arrow pointing, and we pinned it up just inside the gate, showing the way to the garden shed.

Ann said we should want something to put the money in, so she fetched a Pyrex dish and put it on the table on the Paisley shawl, and the Bring and Buy Sale was ready and it looked really elegant.

By now we were starving, so we went inside and ate the cold lunch that Mummy had left and washed up the plates and things, and then there was still about an hour, so we practised Musical Chairs a bit with Black Boy in the orchard. We both had our jodhpurs on, and clean shirts.

At ten minutes to two we washed our hands and brushed our hair and went and stood behind the table in the shed, most frightfully excited to see what would happen and if anybody would come.

'I'll die if nobody comes,' said Ann.

'Oh!' I said. 'Do they sometimes have a Bring and Buy Sale and nobody comes?'

'Oh, no,' said Ann reassuringly. 'Heaps of people come always. Only I suppose I just got the needle because this is our own affair.'

'Help!' I said. 'I believe somebody's coming.'

'It's old Miss Acheson,' said Ann. 'She's frightfully benevolent and always goes to all the Bring and Buy Sales.'

Miss Acheson was about eighty and very short-sighted. She peered at Ann, and said, 'Good afternoon, my dear. I came early because I have to go on to the Girl Guides' display. I've brought you this' – and she laid a brown paper parcel on the table.

She looked a bit surprised when she saw the table was bare.

'Oh dear!' she said. 'It is a Sale, isn't it?'

'You're the first,' said Ann. 'We haven't got anything to sell yet.'

'Oh, what a pity,' said Miss Acheson. 'Still, it can't be helped. Good afternoon.' And away she went.

'That's a bit awkward,' said Ann. 'Anyway, now we've got something to sell, if anybody else comes'; and she opened Miss Acheson's parcel which contained a home-made wool scarf knitted in a rather poisonous shade of green.

We laid this out on the table.

Just then I saw another lady come in at the gate.

'It's Mrs Newton,' said Ann.

'Hello, Ann,' said Mrs Newton, looking rather surprised. 'I didn't know this was one of your mother's efforts?'

'Well, it isn't exactly,' said Ann.

'I've brought you a bottle of my home-made chutney,' said Mrs Newton. 'I suppose I'll have to buy something. What have you got?'

'Well, it's a bit early,' said Ann. 'We've only got this scarf.'

'Oh, I don't want that,' said Mrs Newton. 'Perhaps I'll come back later, if I have time.'

So she said good-bye and went.

'Now we've got two things to sell,' said Ann.

'But we haven't taken any money yet,' I pointed out.

'I say!' said Ann, unscrewing the top of the bottle of chutney. 'This chutney smells pretty awful. I hope it hasn't gone bad.'

'Well, screw it up tight,' I said, 'and let's hope that somebody will buy it without smelling it.'

Presently an elderly gentleman and lady came in. I didn't know them and neither did Ann.

The lady said, 'We always believe in supporting all the local efforts.'

She put down a parcel on the table, and picked up the chutney and said, 'How much is this?'

Ann looked blank, because actually we had forgotten to talk about prices.

'Five pence,' I said wildly.

'All right, I'll have it,' said the elderly lady. 'You don't seem to have much to sell yet, do you?'

I put the proceeds in the Pyrex dish, feeling frightfully bucked that we were actually raising money at last. Ann opened the parcel and disclosed a bag of rather greasy-looking buns and a shaving mug with A PRESENT FROM BOURNEMOUTH on it. We put the mug next to the green scarf and arranged the buns round. The table began to look pretty good.

Then there was a lull and for ages nobody came at all. We both felt very low. Then about three o'clock, five people arrived all at once. Actually they had brought rather nice things, like gardening gloves and quarter-pounds of tea, so they all bought each other's things, and when they had gone away there were forty-three pence in the Pyrex dish, and we still had the buns and the shaving mug and the green scarf.

'Gosh!' I said. 'It's getting exciting.'

Then something even more exciting happened. A car drew up at the gate and a chauffeur got out and came walking up the path carrying something in his hand.

He said, 'Mrs Sullivan sends her compliments and is very sorry she can't attend the Bring and Buy Sale as she has a previous engagement, but she asked me to bring you this.'

'This,' was a little straw punnet filled with paper shavings, and on the shavings there sat six lovely brown eggs.

Then for about half an hour we were most frightfully busy, and when the smoke, as you might say, cleared from the battle-field I found that Ann had sold the eggs for fifteen pence, the buns for five pence and the green

scarf for four pence, and I had sold the shaving mug for
two pence, and there was somehow or other one pound
and sixty-nine pence in the Pyrex dish, and on the table
was a bundle of rhubarb and a dog collar and a book
called *What to Do till the Doctor Comes*.

Then a small girl of about seven came in and said her
Mummy had sent her to buy something, so we sold her
the book for two and a half pence and the dog collar for
ten pence, and as her Mummy had given her fifteen pence
to spend we said she could have the rhubarb for two
and a half pence.

That cleared us out, and made the money in the Pyrex
dish up to one pound eighty-four pence.

Nobody else seemed to be coming and I was nearly
dying of thirst, so I went into the house for a drink of
water, and as Ann said she wasn't thirsty she stayed
outside in case any more customers came.

Unfortunately I managed to break the glass I was

drinking out of, and it took me a long time to sweep up all the pieces. When I went outside again, Ann said, 'I say, I hope you don't mind but I've sold the Paisley shawl.'

'Oh,' I said, feeling a bit taken back.

'I got an awful lot for it,' said Ann. 'A pound. A man came with a little cart, and I said, "I'm afraid we haven't got anything left to sell," and he said, "Well, what about this?" and I said, "Well, actually it belongs to Jill's mother," and he said, "I'll give you a pound for it," so I thought you'd be pleased, and I said O.K. Oh, and he gave me five pence for the Pyrex dish, so that more or less clears us out, and we've made one pound – no, *two* pounds eighty-nine. I've counted it.'

'I hope to goodness you haven't sold the kitchen table,' I said, 'as we haven't got another.'

'Oh no,' said Ann. 'It's still here.'

So actually there was very little clearing up to do after the Bring and Buy Sale. We just carried the kitchen table in, and put the tools back in the shed, and took the notices down; and then we made a plate of jam sandwiches and had tea.

Ann said, another time we'd arrange tea for the customers, as her mother said that always made a lot of money.

Talking of money made me realize that after all we hadn't made forty pounds and that anything we had made, namely two pounds eighty-nine pence, would have to be shared with Ann, as it had been her idea and she had done quite half the work. So I said we had better share fifty-fifty, but Ann said no, the sale had been at our house and therefore I ought to have the most, so she would just take a pound towards the portable radio she was saving up for, which left me with one pound eighty-nine pence.

After she had gone home, which was at half past five, I began to feel a bit funny about this, as such a lot of it had come from Mummy's Paisley shawl and our Pyrex dish, and I began to think that perhaps Bring and Buy Sales were not so profitable after all as a means of raising money.

When Mummy did get home I was quite glad to pour out the whole story to her, only I will now draw a veil, as the storm burst. It was awful, because though in a way I had been quite innocent, Mummy pointed out to me that Bring and Buy Sales are always in aid of some charitable object such as orphans or missionaries, and never, never in aid of Yourself.

She said I would have to make a list of all the people who had been to our sale, and what they had spent and go and give it back to them, and see that Ann did too. And when I told her about the Paisley shawl she went quite white, because it had belonged to her great-grandmother, and though it was worth a great deal more than a pound it was what they call the sentimental value which counted most.

To make a long story short, Ann and I did give the money back, though some people were very decent and laughed and wouldn't take it, as they said they had enjoyed our Bring and Buy Sale so much it was worth whatever it was they had spent.

Next day Mummy went to the police, and they found the man with the cart and made him take the pound and five pence back and give up the Paisley shawl and the Pyrex dish.

Thus ended our Bring and Buy Sale and my efforts to raise money. In the end, of course, it was Martin who came to the rescue once again. He had heard the story somewhere, and he said, 'Surely you didn't think I would enter you for a gymkhana and not turn you out properly? Our stables are full of saddles and what not, and I'd have offered you a better saddle for Black Boy long ago, only you're so proud and always talking about silly things like obligations that don't exist.'

So his man brought the saddle, and Mummy said it was a lot more than I deserved.

# 14 - Camp Pegasus

WILL you believe me? – in less than a week I was in trouble again. Mummy came in one day with that tight, saving-it-up look on her face, and at lunch time out it came.

'Jill, I hear that you refused an invitation from Mrs Harvey some time ago, without consulting me? How was that?'

I thought furiously for a minute, and then remembered how in the autumn Mrs Harvey had invited me to go for a riding week-end to a farm and I had refused without telling Mummy because it cost eight pounds.

So I just said rather cautiously, 'Oh.'

'I don't know what "oh" means,' said Mummy crossly. 'But I think you were very rude. You know how I detest casualness. It was most ungrateful to Martin too. Why on earth didn't you tell me about it at the time?'

'I don't know,' I mumbled.

'And that is no answer,' said Mummy. 'Really, Jill, you get worse and worse.'

'O.K.,' I said, and got up from the table shrugging my shoulders in a pretty awful sort of way, only I didn't mean it a bit like that. I went up to my room and stood staring out of the window, feeling like those noble people in history, Joan of Arc and others, who were misunderstood. They may have got a kick out of it but I didn't.

Mummy didn't come near me and the afternoon

dragged along. It was awful. At four o'clock I couldn't bear it any longer; besides, I was jolly hungry, so I went down and said, 'I didn't tell you about it because it cost eight pounds and I'm sick of being noble. In future I'm going to be an adventuress.' And I grabbed Black Boy's tin off the sink and went out of the back door.

Mummy came after me and we had a reconciliation, and went back for tea.

'The fact is,' said Mummy, 'that Mrs Harvey and Eileen have sent you another invitation of the same kind. They are getting up a party to spend a week at a farm in Warwickshire, and they wondered if you would like to go and take two friends. I want you to go, Jill, so if you like the idea we'll call it settled.'

'Oh, how marvellous!' I fairly shouted. 'How absolutely wizard, super, and smashing.'

'I thought you'd like it,' said Mummy. 'You'd better go round and tell Ann, because I presume she'll be one of the two you want to ask.'

Black Boy was ready for some exercise, so I changed, saddled him, and went charging off to the Derry's house. Mrs Derry said that Ann could go, though she fussed a lot about whether the farm would have proper sanitation, and I said I didn't know but I was sure that Mrs Harvey would be most frightfully sanitary wherever she went.

Then Ann and I started discussing who else we would ask, and after going through practically the whole school we finally decided to ask Diana Bush from our form, who was a very decent sort of person and rode quite well too.

At last the great day came, and at tea-time our party arrived at Applegate Farm. The very look of it was exciting. The house was very old, Tudor in fact, and had gables and twisty chimneys, and odd little windows with ivy framing them, and a romantic appearance which made you think of highwaymen and lovelocks and things.

The stableyard, however, was far from antique, it was most beautifully modern and clean and spacious, and there were loose boxes for the horses who were as excited as we were and all snorting and whiffling with pleasure at being in such a nice place and in each other's company, for horses like being in parties as well as people do.

Mr and Mrs Cave who kept the farm were most welcoming, and knew Mrs Harvey well, in fact Mrs Cave had been Eileen's nurse. We all sat down to tea, which consisted of ham and eggs and stewed rhubarb and real cream and very fruity fruit cake; and then Mrs Harvey said, 'Now all to saddle, girls! Let's go and explore.'

Our first ride was one I shall never forget; everything looked and smelt so fresh and lovely. I don't know what sort of holidays are taken by people who read this book, but actually there is no holiday on earth to compare with a riding holiday, and I speak from a wide experience as I have been to Torquay and to the Lake District and other so-called popular places.

Our party consisted of Mrs Harvey, who was about forty but not too old to enjoy life, and a friend of hers about the same age called Mrs Mason who was the best person at telling campfire stories I ever heard. Then there was Eileen Harvey, and a friend of hers – also nineteen – called Gail Dunham; and Eileen's two cousins, Jean and Peta Graham who were fifteen and thirteen, and Ann and Diana and me. Nine in all.

Our sleeping arrangements were great fun, for we slept in two enormous attics which went right across the farmhouse. One had four beds and the other had five.

The four older people slept in one, and we five younger ones in the other, which was just like a school dorm., with iron beds covered with patchwork quilts. The roof of our bedroom sloped down nearly to the floor, and every time you sat up in bed there was a slight crack as your skull hit the roof. After a bit we got used to this. There was a funny dormer window, too, that you had to stand on tiptoe to look out of.

The first night, though we were tired out, none of us could sleep for toffee, and we kept bouncing up in bed and saying, 'Oh!' as our heads cracked on the roof, and then saying, 'Help! I *can't* go to sleep!' This seemed to go on for hours, but at last one by one we all fell asleep from sheer exhaustion. I only seemed to have been asleep a minute when I woke to find Ann shaking me, and it was six o'clock and the sun was simply pouring in at the dormer window, and we all got up and did a war dance at the prospect of a lovely day.

In about ten minutes we were all dressed, though we had to queue up to wash at the one big china wash-bowl with red roses on it, and then out we dashed to do our ponies. We then ate an enormous breakfast, and by nine o'clock were on the road for an all-day ride.

When we got back at night we were all full of fresh air and sunshine and nearly dropping asleep in our saddles, but Mrs Harvey put us through the full routine of rubbing down and feeding our ponies before we ourselves collapsed gratefully in the Caves' hospitable kitchen. Though Mrs Harvey was the greatest fun, she never allowed one minute's slackness or laziness in the jobs we had to do, which was quite right, because if you are slack you will never make a rider, nor will your pony do you credit, and that won't be the pony's fault.

At night we had great fun. It was lovely warm weather, and down at the bottom of the orchard we made a campfire and all sat round it, roasting potatoes and telling stories, mostly about horses, but some about dogs and about children of other countries.

Mrs Harvey produced a scarlet pennon which she fastened to a staff and fixed up beside our campfire, and on the pennon Eileen had embroidered the words Camp Pegasus in white because that was what the Harveys always called their camps, Pegasus being the loveliest horse in any story that has ever been written.

On the fourth day of our holiday Mrs Harvey, Mrs Mason, Eileen, and Gail went to spend the day with some friends, and the rest of us decided to go for a ride by ourselves to visit a ruined castle. However, we didn't get as far as the castle, because we had just clattered through a rushing stream when Ann called out, 'Wait! I've dropped my watch in the stream.'

'Oh, how did you do that?' said Jean, who was given to making pointless remarks.

'The strap was loose. I felt it drop off,' said Ann, giving Jean an exasperated look.

'You ought to have got a new strap,' said Jean infuriatingly.

'Well, I'm going back to look for it,' said Ann, plunging Seraphine back into the stream which wasn't very deep and had a gravelly bottom. We all went in too, to help Ann, but unfortunately the ponies stirred up the bottom and the water went all pink and sandy so we couldn't see anything.

'If you'd all get out,' said Ann, 'I might have a chance.'

Just then Peta Graham who was on the bank a little

farther downstream called out, 'There's something bright here. Perhaps the current's carried it down.'

'Right-ho,' said Ann, 'I'm coming.'

She turned Seraphine to the place where Peta was pointing, but the stream was much wider here and also much deeper, and what was worse it had a mud bottom, and the next minute Seraphine was stuck and floundering madly about trying to pull her feet out and going deeper and deeper in. The mud was all churned up, and the more Seraphine struggled the worse she was caught.

'Can't you keep her still?' said Jean.

'Don't be an idiot,' said Ann. 'It's as much as I can do to stick on her. Can't one of you get in and lead her out?'

'I will,' said Diana, 'but I'll have to take off my jodhpurs.'

So she took off her jodhpurs and she was wearing her gym briefs underneath, and she got down into the stream which came well above her knees, and got hold of Seraphine's bridle and pulled like mad, but it wasn't the slightest use. The next minute Diana was stuck too, and she let go of Seraphine's bridle and sat down with a plop. Then she scrambled out to the bank, oozing mud all over the place and spitting it out of her mouth.

'Goodness, you are a help!' said Ann to the rest of us. 'Jean, yours is the strongest pony. Bring him close to the bank and give me hold of his reins. That's right. Now start him forward quickly!'

With Ann holding on to his reins, Jean gave Bullet, her pony, a hard thwack, and off he went with a will. The next minute Ann came right over Seraphine's head, slap into the water, while Bullet went loping away into the distance.

We started to shriek with laughter.

'Well, of all the mutts!' said Ann witheringly, dragging her dripping form up the bank.

'It's all your own fault,' said Jean. 'You ought to have hung on to Seraphine. I took it for granted you'd do that. Mutt yourself!'

'Look, there's a farm over there,' I said. 'Let's go and see if they'll lend us a strong horse to pull Seraphine out.'

The rest thought this was a good idea, so Peta and I set off to the farm while Jean stayed with the soaking Ann and Diana to keep their morale up.

'And hurry up!' shouted Ann. 'I'm freezing to death!'

The only person we could find at the farm was a deaf old man of about ninety, and it took us ten minutes shouting at the top of our voices to make him understand what we wanted. When he finally understood he told us that all the men and horses were out working in the fields, but we could borrow old Bingo if we liked. He pointed to where old Bingo was standing beside the horse trough with his eyes shut, apparently sound asleep.

Old Bingo was an enormous Suffolk Punch who looked about thirty years old and had a large white moustache and beard.

'Could we have him harnessed?' said Peta.

'He ain't no use for no fancy ridin',' said the old man.

'No, no!' we yelled. 'We want him *harnessed*, with long *traces*, to pull a pony out of the stream.'

'He ain't much good at pullin', ain't Bingo,' said the old man. However he eventually found a set of harness, mostly tied together with string, and we got it on Bingo, and we knotted up the traces. We had to keep waking Bingo up, as he fell asleep again as soon as he was left alone for a minute.

We led him out of the farmyard at last, while the old

man stood looking after us and shaking his head as though he thought we were all going to our doom.

When we got back to our friends, they were standing in a row looking very blue and regarding Seraphine who was also standing, shivering, with the muddy water swirling round her hocks.

'What's that you've got?' said Diana. 'I bet it was in the Ark.'

'You wait,' I said. 'Here, Ann and Diana, you're wet already, so you'd better get in and tie these traces to Seraphine's girths. And tie them tight, for goodness sake.'

'It'll be a scream if Seraphine pulls Bingo in,' said Peta.

'You really do think of the funniest things!' I said witheringly.

It took Ann and Diana about ten minutes to get Bingo's traces tied with reef knots to Seraphine's girths, and they used all the bits of string we could lay our hands on in the process. Meanwhile Bingo went calmly off to sleep again.

'Now!' said Ann at last. 'You three get at Bingo's head, and Diana and I will get behind Seraphine. When I say Go! you give Bingo a good slosh on the flank, Jean, while Jill and Peta pull at his bridle. That ought to get him started. And, Diana, when I say Shove! you shove like billy-ho. Got it?'

'O.K.' we said.

'Right,' said Ann. 'Now – Go! Shove!'

So we all did our part, but Bingo's enormous hoofs only churned about madly as he failed to get a grip on the bank.

'Oh stop!' I shouted, 'or we'll all be in the stream. We'll have to pad his hoofs with something.'

'What with?' said Jean.

'Our jackets,' said Diana. 'It's all we've got. Wrap them round his feet and button them up his legs.'

So we all took off our jackets, except Jean who was wearing a knitted cardigan, and muffled them round Bingo's feet while he looked on, now fully awake, in a very worried way.

Then we all took action stations again.

'Right!' said Ann. 'Now off you go. Go! Shove!'

Bingo's mighty heave astonished us all. The jackets gripped well, and the next minute we all fell flat on our backs while our equine giant went staggering up the bank with Seraphine plunging after.

'She's out,' said Jean.

'You're telling me!' said Ann. 'Gosh, look at our jackets.'

Our jackets were by now just clots of mud, while Peta's and Ann's were very badly torn by Bingo's hind hoofs.

A quarter of an hour later, looking a very sorry crew, we headed back home, wondering what on earth Mrs Harvey would say. But our farmer's wife, Mrs Cave, proved to be a real sport. She didn't go into hysterics or anything when she saw us. She just said, 'Well, we'll have to get you girls straight before Mrs Harvey comes back.' Which was our own idea.

'Just look at our awful jackets!' said Ann.

'That's all right,' said Mrs Cave. 'I'll have those sponged and pressed in no time, and run up the tears on my sewing machine. Now get out of those wet clothes, girls, and in front of my big fire.'

So we all sat in a row with our feet in a kind of pig-trough full of steaming hot water and mustard, and drank cups of boiling Bovril. And Mrs Cave was a real fairy, I do believe, because by the time Mrs Harvey and the others got back we were all clean and clothed again as though nothing had happened.

Mrs Harvey said, 'Have you had a nice day, girls?'

'Oh, marvellous!' said Ann with great presence of mind. 'My pony stuck in a stream but we pulled her out.'

The next day Ann and I went back and found her watch lying quite peacefully in the gravelly part of the stream, and it didn't seem much the worse either. Then we went along to the farm and took a handful of carrots that Mrs Cave had given us for Bingo.

'Bingo's a dear,' said Ann to the farmer. 'You will let

him stay here and have a peaceful old age, won't you?'

'That I will,' said the farmer. 'No old horse that has worked for me shall ever go to them nasty knackers to be made into cat's meat.'

'If I were a millionaire,' I said, 'I'd buy acres and acres of parkland, and fill it with old horses, so that nobody could be cruel to them or sell them to those beastly people on the Continent.'

'You're a couple of grand little horsewomen,' said the farmer.

'Not so little,' growled Ann as we rode away.

So at last Camp Pegasus broke up, though we all agreed we would have liked to stay for ever.

# 15 – A job for Jill

ONE day when I was exercising Black Boy, cantering gaily along the grass verge of a lane and singing to myself in my own peculiar style, I heard someone say, 'Hallo there!' and looked round to see Mrs Darcy who owned the riding school overtaking me astride a raking chestnut of about seventeen hands.

'Grand morning!' she said, and I agreed that it was. Mrs Darcy was the sort of person who always seemed to have an exclamation mark after everything she said; that is why I have put one.

'I've seen you about quite a lot,' she went on. 'You're Jill Crewe, aren't you? That's a good pony, and you've got quite a decent style! *Quite* a decent style!'

'Oh. Thanks,' I said, rather taken back.

'I hope you're spending plenty of time on schooling,' she went on. 'Riding isn't just cantering about the lanes, you know! It's easy, but it isn't equitation!'

'Oh, I know,' I said. 'I put in as much schooling as I can find time for.'

'Soon be gymkhana season!' said Mrs Darcy; and I nodded, feeling a thrill at the magic word, and also at Mrs Darcy's assumption that I should be interested in gymkhanas this season.

'You once came to see me about a job, didn't you?' said Mrs Darcy. 'Let me see, how old are you?'

'Twelve,' I said.

'And you've got sense?'

'I hope so,' I said.

'You groomed your pony yourself this morning?'

I laughed. 'Well, if I didn't, nobody else would.'

'Right! I'm in a bit of a fix. My young groom has broken her arm and will be off work for several weeks, and we're very busy at the stables. If you're in the same mind about doing a job of work, I wonder if you'd care to come and help for an hour or two each day, between school hours? If you're keen on horses, as I think you are, it will be good for you to get stable practice, and hard work never hurt any rider! My father stabled eighteen hunters when I was a kid, and I tell you I put in some honest toil! So what about it?'

The idea of working in the stable fascinated me.

'When would you want me to come?' I asked.

'Well, if you could manage an hour before school in the morning, and an hour or more after –'

'Oh, I think I could do that.'

'I'll pay you fifteen pence an hour, but I mean an hour of work! No leaning against doors, chatting!'

We finally arranged that I should be at Mrs Darcy's every morning from seven to eight o'clock, and every afternoon from five to six-thirty, provided of course that Mummy said I might do it.

I didn't know how Mummy would cotton on to the idea, but I was pretty full of enthusiasm when I put it to her.

'Well,' she said, 'I'm rather keen on initiative, and I don't think a job of work ever hurt anybody. But you'll find it stiff going, Jill. It's easy to start something in the first rush of enthusiasm, but it isn't so easy to keep it up – especially when it involves getting up early every single morning for several weeks. I doubt if you'll stick it.'

'I'll stick it,' I said. 'Only please, Mummy, *say* I can start. I do want to. It will be so marvellous working in a real stable with a lot of horses.'

'If,' said Mummy, 'I find that this is interfering with your school work I shall stop it at once. I shall soon find out if you are dreaming about stables all day instead of thinking about your arithmetic.'

'I won't let it interfere,' I promised.

So the next morning I turned up at Mrs Darcy's in my jeans and an ancient sweater, and my oldest shoes, and I did mucking out while the girl groom, Angela, who was about twenty, did the feeds. Angela was awfully nice, though Mrs Darcy didn't allow talking and there was too much to do in any case.

I went back after afternoon school and cleaned tack on a large scale. Actually the whole time I was working at Mrs Darcy's was just an orgy of mucking out, feeds, grooming, and cleaning tack, and of course I did most of the dirtier work as that was what I was there for. Mrs Darcy was frightfully strict and had an eye like a hawk. She always looked first at all the parts you might have missed if you didn't want to bother. You never stood still a minute, either; she kept you whizzing round.

Mummy was right, it was tough going, especially after the first thrill of realizing that I was actually working in a stable wore off.

I jolly well had to make myself stick it, but my pride was such that I wouldn't slacken off, and after about the first fortnight I got my second wind and felt as though I could go on for ever. I did enjoy the work, and I learned stable practice as it should be learned and how to do things for horses in the professional way. It made me much quicker and defter with my hands. I also picked up lots of new ideas about equitation and schooling. And the money each Saturday came in jolly useful too.

My days were now quite crowded. I set my alarm for half-past-five, and at six I was at work in my own stable. Meanwhile my porridge and egg were on the gas cooker, and I ate my breakfast and biked up the hill to work by seven o'clock. At 8.15 I was home again for a hasty wash and change into my school uniform, and I was at school at ten-to-nine. Afternoon school finished at four; I was home at 4.15, had tea, changed into my working clothes, and was at Mrs Darcy's at five. Home again at 6.45; attended to my own pony; then homework from 7.15 to 8.15; then supper, and I was in bed and asleep by nine. Mummy insisted on this, if I was to get up at 5.30.

You will see that this didn't leave me any time for riding and schooling Black Boy except at week-ends; but to my surprise and pleasure Ann suddenly said that she would come round each afternoon after school to exercise Black Boy and give him a bit of schooling, and this she did, and I thought it very decent of her. Besides, it had a good effect in making Ann much keener on horses generally. The horse is like that; the more you have to do with it, the more you want to.

On Saturdays I did my two and a half hours at the stable, and spent the rest of the day working at my own pony, partly under Martin's instruction. Ann came round every Saturday afternoon, and we had terrific times. We were both getting pretty good now.

Sunday afternoon was a very busy time at the riding school, so I used to go up there from eight to nine in the morning, and then go to church with Mummy; and go back for grooming and cleaning tack in the evening. But

I did this latter because I liked it, for Mummy would not allow me to take money for working on Sunday.

One Saturday, just as I was finishing work, Mrs Darcy called, 'Come here, Jill.'

She was out in the yard, holding a black mare called Inez, the one horse in the stable I did not like, for she had an uncertain temper and rather a grudging nature, but Mrs Darcy frequently rode her and hired her out as a hack to her friends.

'Come along. Let me see you mount,' said Mrs Darcy. 'No use working in a stable if you can't ride the horses!'

I went up to Inez rather reluctantly. For one thing, she was much too big for me, being fifteen-two. The stirrup iron was high, and I had to make two attempts before I could get my foot in it; then I kept hopping and springing, but I couldn't get up, and the more I tried the worse it was.

'Oh, get down!' said Mrs Darcy. 'You're awful. If you messed about like that at a gymkhana they'd disqualify you!'

'Inez is miles too big for me,' I said sulkily.

'Nonsense,' said Mrs Darcy. 'I've seen a child a head shorter than you mount a horse of sixteen hands like a fairy. You don't know everything about riding yet, you see!'

I turned away, rather angry, and was walking back to the stable when she called me.

'Now don't go away in a huff. Come here, and let me see what I can do with you.'

Then to my surprise she spent about half-an-hour on improving my mounting and dismounting, and general style. I was very grateful to her. Mrs Darcy was like that, her bark was worse than her bite. Before I left her, I could ride any horse in her stable. What was more, when my half-term holiday arrived and I had a free Monday and Tuesday, she let me take out a party of children, and also arranged a jolly evening ride for myself and Angela and a few more.

Though my days were long and packed and I hardly had time to breathe, and no time at all for my own affairs, and though Mummy watched me like a lynx to see that my school work didn't suffer from my horsy occupations, I was really quite sorry when Sheila came back and it was time for me to leave Mrs Darcy's. I had learned so much and it had been such fun.

I stayed on for a week after Sheila came, so that she could work her arm in gently, and all the talk was about gymkhanas, and the horses that Angela was going to ride and the novice-jumping events that she hoped to win on Mrs Darcy's horses. It was simply thrilling.

The last evening I was there, they all came to the gate to say good-bye to me, and Mrs Darcy clapped her hand on my shoulder and said, 'Well, I didn't think you'd stick it! But you're welcome here any time! Thanks!' Which was such high praise for her that I nearly collapsed.

# 16 - La Blonde

IT was early summer now, and sunbeams, green leaves, little birds, and gymkhanas were in the air.

At school you heard nothing else, and three girls in my form were sent to the head-mistress for reading gymkhana schedules inside their history books.

'What are we going to enter for?' said Ann one morning at break, waving the schedules of Lentham Park children's pony gymkhana at me. Ann was by now nearly as keen as I was, thanks to Martin's influence and the great friendship between our ponies, Black Boy and Seraphine.

'Well, I haven't got an earthly in the riding classes,' I said. 'And the very thought of the jumping – well, I'm sure people don't enter for the jumping in their very first gymkhana. That only leaves things like Bending and Musical Chairs and Egg and Spoon.'

'There's the cleanest pony,' said Ann, not too hopefully.

'I expect some people will take their ponies in travelling boxes and groom them all over again when they get there,' I said. 'By the time you and I have hacked to Lentham Park, our ponies will look like something out of the farmyard.'

'It's under their saddles and in their ears where the judges look,' said Ann. 'You'll see. Now what *are* we going to enter for?'

'They all scare me stiff,' I said, 'down on paper.' Just

then Susan Pyke came by, and for once she stopped and gave us a patronizing smile.

'Is that the Lentham Park schedule?' she said. 'I know just how you feel. I was the same when I began, feebly reading over all the events I daren't go in for.'

We went on seething for ages after she had gone, and Ann said her only ambition in life was to be about thirty and a famous woman M.F.H. and to order Susan Pyke off the hunting-field for unsportsmanlike behaviour.

However about two days later Susan came up to us and said, would we go home to tea with her that afternoon, and out of sheer curiosity – and after obtaining our mothers' permission at lunch-time – we said we would.

Susan Pyke's house was a rather glassy-looking place with wood floors and antique furniture, and bowls of spiky, uncomfortable hot-house flowers. Susan's mother was majestic and had a deep voice and kept calling us 'children' as if we were six.

'Come in to tea, children! ... Wipe your shoes, children!'

The other two people there were twin sisters from our form called Valeria and Jacqueline Horrington-Hobday-Heath. That really and actually was their name, though at school they were called Val and Jack Heath, and they were quite decent sort of people.

'I hear that all you children are learning to ride,' said Mrs Pyke while we were having tea.

Nobody said anything, there isn't much you can say to a remark like that, except yes.

'Well, you must all work very hard at your riding,' said Mrs Pyke, 'and then one day you may be as good as Susan. Even Susan had to begin once!'

'Golly!' said Ann under her breath, and Mrs Pyke said, 'A little choke, dear? Take a drink – not too quickly.'

'When I was a child,' said Mrs Pyke, 'I was the youngest rider to hounds in the county. I remember the M.F.H. once lifted me on to my pony himself, and there I sat in my little habit with my long fair curls hanging down to my waist. Children had the loveliest hair in those days.'

Personally I thought (*a*) it was impossible to picture Mrs Pyke as a child at all, and (*b*) that curls down to your waist must have looked pretty awful all waving in the breeze like floating cork-screws. I'm sure Mrs Darcy would have had something to say about it. I mean, there are always plaits.

After tea we found out that the object of our visit was to see Susan's cups. They were all set out on the sideboard and they really did look terrific, gleaming and flashing with Goddard's Plate Powder.

'A very nice array,' said Mrs Pyke, and we just said yes. At least Val Heath – who had frightfully good manners – said yes, and then Jack said yes, and then Ann and I said yes too, as the others had said it.

'And now perhaps you'd like to see Susan's certificates,' said Mrs Pyke. 'Get them out, Susan dear.'

I will say to Susan's credit that she went a bit red, but she opened a drawer in the sideboard and there they were. A great big thick pile of red, blue and yellow certificates – mostly red and blue – and not a green one to be seen. Either Susan never condescended to be highly commended, or else she just threw her green ones into the waste paper basket.

Susan was still a bit red, and when she had closed the drawer she said, 'Let's go down to the stables. I've got something to show you. That's why I asked you to come.'

So we all went down to the stables – which I can't describe because they made me so envious, being just the kind of stables I always dreamed of possessing when I was grown up – and Susan opened a door, and there it was.

It was a new pony, and when we saw it we all gave a gasp. It was the showiest Show pony I ever beheld in all my long and varied experience. It was fourteen hands, and it had the most beautiful flowing lines, and it held its head like an Arab steed. In colour it was pale biscuit, gleaming like satin, and its mane and tail though long were perfectly groomed and a sort of soft gold colour.

'Daddy found her for me,' said Susan simply. 'She's called La Blonde.'

'Can't you just *see* Susan on her!' said Mrs Pyke. 'Let's take her in the paddock, children. You must see her action.'

So Susan saddled La Blonde – and all the tack was new – and rode her round the paddock, and did a few perfect figures-of-eight, and changed legs with nonchalant efficiency (excuse those big words, but I have had them written down on a bit of paper for ages waiting until I got a chance to use them. You can look them up in the Dic.). We stood round and watched.

'I got a First in the riding class at Pillton last August,' said Val suddenly. 'Under fourteens.'

I suppose she couldn't bear this 'beginners watching the expert' feeling any longer.

But nobody took any notice, and I don't think Mrs Pyke heard.

On our way home Val said, 'I bet that pony fairly hypnotizes the judges at Lentham Park.'

'It's nothing but a circus pony,' said Jack.

'Oh no, it isn't,' said Ann. 'It really is something special, and I'm sure it's half Arab. I expect Susan's father bought it from a sheik for about fifty thousand pounds.'

'You don't buy things from sheiks,' I pointed out. 'They give you horses for saving their lives.'

'I wouldn't mind saving a sheik's life,' said Val. 'I've done First Aid at the Guides.'

'Well, I don't see any of us getting to Arabia before Lentham Park,' said Ann, 'so we might as well make the best of the ponies we've got, as they're all we'll have. La Blonde! Golly!'

So then we all started giggling and playing a game, and Ann was La Blonde, and I was Susan, and Val was Mrs Pyke-as-a-child, and Jack was the M.F.H. who put her up on her pony; and in the end we were all sitting in a row in the ditch shrieking with laughter.

Next day Martin told us that he had entered Ann and me for all the events at Lentham Park, and it made us feel as though we were going to the dentist's.

For my birthday Mummy had bought me a pair of jodhpur boots and a blue shirt, and Martin's mother had given me a crash cap, and I got everything cleaned and ready in time – for once.

Well, I don't want to go into details about my first gymkhana, because I certainly did not cover myself with glory. I was frightfully nervous, and that ruined everything; and what was worse I communicated my nervousness to my pony – which always happens – so that he didn't behave a bit well, and it was my fault really. So far as I was concerned things went from bad to worse. Ann was much better than me, and got a Third in the riding class under fourteen, and a Second in the bending race under sixteen. My only comfort was that lots of other children were as bad as I was.

It was Susan Pyke's day. When she rode into the ring on La Blonde everybody gave a gasp. She looked marvellous. She had a perfect black jacket and cream cord breeches, and black boots, and a white shirt and yellow tie, and a new hat and cream string gloves.

Just as Ann had said, the judges were hypnotized. I don't think they were very good judges at Lentham Park, because usually judges are the most fair and sporting of people and look for fine points in equitation rather than a showy appearance, but these judges were taken by surprise, and Susan was called in within two minutes and got First in all the showing classes, *and* in the equitation, though even I could see that she had lost her head and was over-riding La Blonde and sawing at her mouth and letting her over-bend. This turned the feeling of the spectators against Susan; and now that I have a long and varied experience of gymkhanas, I do think that the feeling of the crowd towards you can either help or hinder very much.

Whatever La Blonde looked like, she certainly couldn't jump. She just shoved her way through everything, and soon people were laughing, and then there was a roar and Susan went scarlet with rage and began beating La Blonde about the head with her whip, and the next moment the judge had ordered her off the field. Ann and I looked at one another unbelievingly.

However, Susan turned up again in the Musical Chairs, and won the First in the under-fourteens and the Third in the under-sixteens. I think this was partly luck and partly that La Blonde seemed to have a natural gift for Musical Chairs.

When it was over I joined Mummy and Martin and a few of our friends who had been watching, and said, 'I say, I'm sorry I was such a wash-out.'

'Not a bit,' said Martin. 'Whoever heard of anybody doing anything at their first gymkhana? You didn't do a thing wrong, Jill, and you looked very nice and I was proud of you.'

Then Ann came riding up with her rosettes, and quite honestly I was as pleased as if they'd been mine.

When we were on the way home Mummy said, 'I don't believe in giving you a swelled head, Jill, but in case you may be feeling a bit low, I'll tell you that as you rode past I overheard two people behind me say, "I'm surprised that girl in the blue shirt hasn't won anything; I'd say she was the most promising rider of the lot."'

'Oh, you're making it up,' I cried.

But Mummy assured me that this was true.

# 17 - I go on a visit

OF course at school on Monday we had the inquest on the gymkhana. Nobody could talk about anything else but just where they went wrong and what bad luck they had.

Susan Pyke said, 'What do you think? Daddy is going to sell La Blonde. He was simply furious at the way she let me down in the jumping. He says he can't have my chances ruined by a pony like that!'

'I thought your chances were ruined when you started bashing her on the head and the judge ordered you off the field,' Ann could not resist saying.

'Oh, Ann Derry you are a beast,' said Susan, and to our surprise burst into tears, whereupon several of Susan's friends rallied round her and we stood exchanging sarky remarks and insults until the bell went.

It happened to be two days before the exams, and having had a heart-to-heart talk from Mummy I did try very hard to give my mind to such squalid matters as the dissolution of the monasteries, and Thomas Cromwell and Oliver Cromwell being two different persons which was something that always bothered me, particularly as I could never remember which was which even when I got them apart.

I biked home from school intending to swot like anything that night, but somehow my nobler intentions are always frustrated and this was no exception. Mummy was making tea and looking rather blue when I arrived, and presently she said, 'I've just been to the dentist's and I'm afraid I'm going to have to go into the Dental Hospital at Rychester for a few days for a dental operation.'

'Oh, I'm sorry,' I said. 'When?'

'About Thursday.' Mummy gave a watery smile, and added, 'I don't know how it is, but dental operations always sound so sordid. In books, people's mothers have such romantic things the matter with them, in pink marabout bed-jackets. I'm sorry I couldn't oblige with anything but teeth. But the point is, Jill, something has to be done about you.'

'Oh, that's all right,' I said. 'I can manage here perfectly well by myself.'

'I wouldn't think of leaving you here by yourself,' said Mummy.

(I don't know where parents get the idea that people over ten years old can't manage the house as well as they can, but they are all like this.)

I argued a bit, but it wasn't any use. Then Mummy said something that sent an icy chill through my bones. She said, 'I'm glad that we had Cecilia to stay in the Christmas holidays because I don't feel any compunction now in asking them to take you. In fact I rang up this afternoon when I was in Chatton, and they'll be very glad to see you at White Ferry' – which was the misleading name of Cecilia's house, as it wasn't white and there wasn't a ferry within miles of it – 'and I'm sure that Farmer Clay will put your pony up while you're away. So that'll be all right,' concluded Mummy, in a deathly silence through which nothing could be heard but my madly-beating heart.

'Oh, Mummy!' I cried, and my voice went all up and down and wobbled. 'Don't make me go to Cecilia's. I couldn't! I should die! I'd go into a decline or have a stroke or something. Not Cecilia's! Couldn't I go to the Derrys'? I'm sure Ann –'

'No, you can't,' said my hard-hearted parent. 'I don't know Mrs Derry well enough to be under such an obligation to her. You must go to your cousin's, so don't be so silly. It's the obvious thing.'

'Oh, Mummy!' I wailed. 'Let me go to Mrs Darcy's. I could sleep in the hay-loft. She wouldn't mind. Please!'

'Go and wash your face, darling,' said Mummy. 'It's all settled, and anyway it's only for five days or so.'

'People can die in five days,' I said grimly, 'when they're in durance vile.'

Tea was a very damp sort of meal, and when it was over I put my mac on and went for a walk. I wandered stonily along the lanes, feeling as though the end of the world had come, I was so miserable. I think now that I must have been pretty selfish, too, not to have been thinking of Mummy and her beastly dental operation, than which I cannot imagine anything worse happening to a person. It makes me go cold all over when I am just going to have a tooth filled. But I wasn't thinking of poor Mummy at all, only of myself and what I should suffer at Cecilia's.

And then as I kicked a stone along the road before me, there suddenly came the most beautiful thought. The exams began on Wednesday! And with Mummy so keen on the exams, how could I possibly be away at Cecilia's? I couldn't! It was just like Hetty Sorrel in Adam Bede when the rider comes dashing through the crowd crying, 'A reprieve! A reprieve!'

I jumped right up in the air, and yelled, 'Yippee! Yoicks! Tally-ho! Gone awa-a-a-a-a-y!'

'Dear, dear!' said a voice behind me. 'The girl has gone quite mad.'

I looked round, and there in her carriage with the matched greys was Martin's mother, Mrs Lowe.

'I thought it was you, Jill,' she said. 'Whatever has happened?'

So I poured the whole story into her sympathetic ear, and when I had finished she said, 'But of course you must come and stay with us while your mother is away. And bring your pony too, there's lots of room. Tell your mother I won't take a refusal, and I'll see that you go to school every day at the proper time.'

I was so relieved and happy that I rushed home and poured this all out to Mummy in a breathless jumble, and though of course she wanted to say a lot about obligations and so on, she saw my point about the exams, and actually she was in what is known as a cleft stick.

I was thrilled at the prospect of going to stay at Martin's home, though I must say that when the actual moment came and the taxi was at the door to take Mummy to the hospital I did feel perfectly awful. I mean, it is a most shattering feeling to see your beloved home being locked up and your dearly loved mother being dragged away to a squalid hospital while you yourself are turned out into the cold world, and I hope nobody who reads this book will ever have this experience.

When the taxi was out of sight and there wasn't anything left to wave to, I felt like leaning my face up against my pony and having a good howl, but I managed to strangle this feeling and, without a backward glance at the locked and desolate cottage, I mounted and rode towards my new home.

Gradually my spirits rose as I thought of the good time

I was going to have at The Grange. It would be fun
staying with the Lowes, and being made much of, and
riding all those horses.

When I came in sight of the drive gates, there was
Martin waiting for me.

'I thought I'd be on the look-out,' he said. 'Welcome,
Jill. I hope you'll treat us as if you belonged here for the
next few days. And cheer up, it won't be for long.'

'Thanks most awfully,' I said.

I led Black Boy up the drive beside Martin as he
propelled himself along in his chair.

'There's one treat in store for you,' he went on, 'you'll
have some good company of near your own age. Two
young cousins of mine, Pierce and Mary Lowe, have
come to stay. They're twins of sixteen, and their school
have broken up a bit in advance of yours – in fact Mary
goes to school in Paris. They're both grand riders and
will be able to show you a lot.'

All the way up the drive he went on talking about
Pierce and Mary, telling me what marvellous people they
were, so consequently by the time we arrived at the front
door I was certain I was going to hate them, and all the
pleasant anticipation of my visit had oozed out of my
shoes. It is a funny thing, but whenever your friends tell
you how much you are going to like some wonderful
people they know, you always start hating them on the
spot.

Martin showed me into the dining-room and at once
my worst fears were realized.

Pierce and Mary, who were standing by the window
looking at some snapshots of the Lowe horses, were
very tall and grown up. Mary, who had just come in from
a ride, was a typical hard woman to hounds, while Pierce

had the supercilious look worn by boys who are nearly men.

'Meet Mary and Pierce!' cried Martin. 'This is Jill whom I told you about – another doughty horse-woman.'

Both the twins said, 'How-d'y'do'; then Pierce gave me a bored glance and looked away, closing his eyes as though he couldn't bear the sight; while Mary just looked at me and then at Martin, as much as to say, 'Need we be bothered with the infant class?'

'Just take Jill up to her room, Mary, that's a good chap,' said Martin; and Mary said, 'Certainly. Please come this way.'

So I followed her up the stairs, and she marched on without saying anything, finally opening the door of a pretty white-panelled bedroom.

'This is yours,' she said. 'Tea is at four. Don't be late, please.'

With this she left me alone, and I sat down on the end of the bed feeling like one of those unfortunate people

whose relatives put them into a Home. I looked at my watch, which said half past three, and wondered if I was supposed to stay in my bedroom until tea. Apparently I was. For something to do I unpacked my suitcase, and put into the drawers my dreary and dejected-looking garments which, in addition to my riding-clothes, consisted of two clean school blouses, my best shoes, a navy-blue dress with a white collar which made me look about ten, and some underwear.

At last a silvery gong sounded and I went down to tea, which took place in the drawing-room. Mr and Mrs Lowe were there and gave me a very nice welcome, except that they would talk about Mummy in that prepare-for-the-worst way that some grown-ups do when anyone is ill. Then the conversation became all about people I didn't know and Pierce and Mary did, so I felt rather like that feeble game where people throw a tennis ball back and forth above your head and you have to jump and try to catch it as it whizzes over you, which is practically impossible and very maddening.

I thought somebody might suggest a ride after tea, but nobody did, so I wandered out to the loose boxes and saw that Black Boy was being most beautifully looked after, and he gave me a smug look as if to say, Home was never like this.

Then Mrs Lowe called me in and reminded me that she had promised Mummy I should do my homework, so I sat down in a little morning-room which she said I could have all to myself, and began to swot up geometry, as it was the geometry exam next day.

Dinner was as bad as tea, except that they all talked in a very magazine-ish way about Paris, and my only hope was that any moment somebody would say *Pas devant l'enfant*, in which case I was going to say something very sophisticated and crushing, but the opportunity never came.

After dinner Mary said to Mrs Lowe, 'Do you mind very much if Pierce and I dash off to catch the bus? There's rather a good film in Chatton.'

But instead of saying, 'Yes, of course, and take Jill with you,' Mrs Lowe made the humiliating remark, 'Well, don't be too late, dears; and Jill must go straight to bed now, because I promised her Mummy that school work should come first.'

All I could think of in that moment was that it served me right for not going to Cecilia's.

But worse was to follow.

The sun shining on my face woke me at seven next morning, and I bounded out of bed, dragged on my faded old dressing-gown – which I had when I was nine and which by now only came to my knees with the sleeves half-way up my arms – and dashed to the bathroom. But I arrived at the same moment as Mary, who was wearing a very smart tailored dressing-gown of brown satin with white spots, and we both grabbed hold of the door-handle together.

Feeling conscious of my awful appearance, I gasped in what I hoped was a nonchalant way, 'Oh, you have it; I won't bother about a bath.' She raised her eyebrows and gave me a very superior look, and as I rushed back to my room I realized that she must be thinking I was a grubby little kid who was glad of an excuse not to have a bath.

This sickening thought pursued me all the time I was dressing, and at last, though I had done my hair and got my blouse and tunic on, I was mad enough to take everything off again and get back into my pyjamas and dressing-gown. Then I seized my towels and marched along to the bathroom, and in order to show Mary that I wasn't in the least afraid of her, I banged heartily on the bathroom door and shouted, 'Hurry up, you! This is Jill, and I want a bath when you've done.'

To my horror Mr Lowe's voice replied, 'Don't be in such a hurry, young lady. You must learn to wait for your elders.'

I just choked, tore back to my room and flung my clothes on anyhow. At breakfast I couldn't say a word, and my misery was added to by Mrs Lowe making such kind but misguided remarks as, 'Do you always eat so little breakfast, Jill dear? If it isn't what you have at home you've only to ask. Don't worry about Mummy, dear, she'll soon be better.'

Martin just looked awkward, and the twins ate and ate and ignored me. I got to school and made an awful mess of the geometry exam, making such howlers as 'A right-angled triangle is one in which all the angles are right-angles' – which was read out to the class later by Miss Greaves.

During exam time we did not have afternoon school, so I went back to the Lowes in time for lunch.

During lunch Mary and Pierce kept saying what a grand day it was for a ride, so my spirits lifted a bit, and when we had finished eating I followed them to the loose boxes in time to see them leading out two magnificent hunters, just the sort of horses they *would* own. Mary – who was beautifully turned out in full hunting kit – had a shining bay mare of about fifteen-two, while Pierce's horse was a light roan with black mane and tail, very tall, lean, and long-legged.

I said nothing, but led out Black Boy who had been

groomed to perfection by Martin's man, Bob, and looked a dear.

'Oh, what a sweet little pony!' said Mary, trying to be nice, and making me feel as if I were five and about to be lifted on to my first Shetland.

'O.K.?' I said, shrugging my shoulders, and then mounting with what I hoped was a sophisticated air.

'I say,' said Pierce, 'you're not expecting to go with us by any chance? I mean, we're going over some pretty fierce country. I mean, you'd find the going much too much.'

'Oh, I don't want to go,' I said carelessly. 'I've got lots of schooling to do.'

So they rode off, and I went and lowered all the jumps in the field and then put Black Boy round them rather dispiritedly and we made an awful mess of it, so that Mr Lowe who happened to be watching from a window banged on the glass and put his head out and shouted, 'No, no! All wrong!'

Though it was only three days from the day I arrived until Saturday it seemed like a year. Mary and Pierce ignored me, and Martin seemed so dense, as though he thought I was actually having a good time with them. I hated them so much that I almost loved Susan Pyke by comparison, and I hated the way they obviously pitied Martin. Mary was always saying things like, 'Let me help you round the corner,' in the way that he had told us he loathed.

Saturday dawned with a pouring wet morning, and we all had to stay indoors. Pierce read a pile of copies of *Horse and Hound*, and Mary chatted to Mr Lowe in a very affected way about bloodstock sales. Nobody bothered about me, so at last I slipped out to the stables to have a word with Black Boy. I would have enjoyed cleaning tack, or anything homely and squalid, but it had all been expertly done by Bob. Even then I couldn't get away from Mrs Lowe who came to fetch me in out of the wet.

The one bright spot was that I was going to see Mummy in the afternoon, so directly lunch was over I dashed off to get the bus to Rychester, which is about twenty miles away. When I got to Rychester, I found I had thirty pence as well as my return bus fare, so I bought some flowers to take to Mummy.

When I eventually got to the hospital I collapsed thankfully on Mummy's bed like a desert traveller at an oasis. She looked a bit pallid and her voice was croaky, but it was Mummy all right.

'Oh when are you coming home?' I gasped. 'It's been like a hundred years.'

She looked surprised.

'But aren't you having a marvellous time at the Lowes?'

'Oh, Mummy, its truly awful,' I said. And then I told her about Pierce and Mary.

'They just ignore me,' I said, 'and everybody treats me as though I were about six – even Martin. They're so superior, and the Lowes treat them as if they were grown-up, and I hate them – I loathe them!'

'Jill,' said Mummy, 'I think you're very feeble.'

'Feeble?' I gasped.

'Yes, feeble to let yourself get an inferiority complex just because two people a bit older than yourself manage to gain some of the attention which you think ought to be exclusively yours,' croaked Mummy. 'Why don't you buck up and be yourself?'

'But they're beastly,' I said. 'Oh, Mummy, are you coming home on Monday? I don't like it a bit at the Lowes.'

Mummy looked grave.

'Jill dear, you make it very difficult for me to say this. I have to tell you that they couldn't complete the operation last Thursday. I have to have another one on Monday, so it will be about Friday before I can go home.'

I looked at her, dumb with horror.

She went on, 'As soon as I knew this, I asked the doctor to phone Mrs Lowe for me, and to say that if it was imposing too much on her kindness to keep you I would make arrangements for you to go on to Cecilia's. Mrs Lowe replied that she would be delighted to have you stay longer, and that you were having a lovely time.'

'Lovely time!' I interrupted. 'Gosh! *Lovely time!*'

'I asked Mrs Lowe not to tell you what had happened,' went on Mummy calmly, 'as I preferred to tell you myself today. I thought you would have been pleased to stay.'

'Of course if you *want* me to go into a decline!' I said bitterly.

'Self-pity *is* painful,' said Mummy, 'and I'm sorry for Mrs Lowe for having had to cope with you. You can't have been very cheery company. You had better arrange to go to Cecilia's tomorrow.'

'That's even worse,' I said with a groan.

'If anyone had asked me,' said Mummy, 'I should have said you were a nice, natural, friendly person who could fit in anywhere. If Pierce and Mary really are nasty, all the more reason for you to be the same Jill that the Lowes have always liked, instead of smouldering in the background. But if you can't take it, then you'll just *have* to go away and miss the rest of the exams. It's my fault for landing in this silly hospital.'

'O.K.,' I grumbled. 'I can take it. I'll stay at the Lowes.'

'That's a relief,' said Mummy with a sigh.

'I do think you might sympathize with me a bit,' I said.

'People with inferiority complexes need bracing, not sympathy,' said Mummy briskly. 'Poor old Jill! Friday will soon come. How's Black Boy? Tell me you've had some riding.'

'A bit,' I said grudgingly. 'By the way, I brought these flowers for you.'

'Oh, how lovely!'

Just then the nurse came in and said it was time for me to go, so I kissed Mummy and went out again into the cold world. It was raining. I felt awful. And then suddenly I realized that I was probably the most awful beast that had ever existed since the beginning of the world. I hadn't asked Mummy how she was, or said how sorry I was about her having to have another operation, or done anything but grouse about myself. I rushed back to the hospital, but the door was shut. I banged on it, and when a nurse came and opened it I said, 'I want to come in again, I've forgotten something.'

She only said coldly, 'I'm sorry, visiting hours are over. The wards are closed now.'

Weary, worn, and sad, I caught the bus and crawled back to my inhospitable lodging.

I expect by now you are saying, 'Well, of all the soppy, feeble little beasts –!' and you are quite right. I was in that silly mood of self-pity in which I should have been quite glad if they had forgotten to keep me any tea. Instead of that I found a huge fire – in spite of it being so-called summer – and Mrs Lowe made me sit right in front of it and brought me a tray with smoking hot buttered toast in a silver dish, and strawberry jam, and cake with marzipan on top, and *Mary* poured my tea out and put heaps of sugar in it, and they said things like, 'You poor woman! You must be drowned!' and other self-respecting remarks. It was like a dream and I was quite dazed.

In the evening Mrs Lowe and Mary went out to visit friends, and by some chance I found myself alone with Pierce. He looked at me very self-consciously, and I thought I would remove my revolting self from his presence, but suddenly he said, 'I say – do you think this is any good?' And he handed me a painting of a pony. It was a grey with a tossing mane, standing on a hill-top against a windy blue sky with racing clouds.

'It's super, isn't it? Who did it?' I asked.

He blushed.

'Well, as a matter of fact, I did. That's why I asked you. I wanted to try it on somebody impartial. I mean, Mary or Martin would have tried to be polite about it whether they meant it or not.'

'I think it's absolutely wizard,' I said, because it really was. 'It's as good as Morland or any of those people.'

'Oh, I say, come off it!' he said. 'What do you know about Morland anyway, at your age.'

'Why, how old do you think I am?' I said.

'Oh, about ten – eleven perhaps,' he added hastily, seeing my look of indignation.

'I'm practically thirteen,' I said. 'Gosh, it's not much younger than you. I bet you can remember being thirteen.'

'Yes, I can,' he said, quite humbly. 'I want to be a painter of horses, only I'm so nervous about my work. I keep thinking I'm no good.'

'*You* think you're no good?' I said in amazement. 'I thought you were so frightfully clever and conceited you knew everything!'

'*Me* clever and conceited!' he said opening his eyes. 'Gosh, no.'

'Then Mary is,' I said, flinging discretion to the winds. 'She's so frightfully superior that she makes me feel as if I could crawl under a blade of grass. I'm terrified of you both, if you want to know; and even if you are sixteen you're not all that marvellous. I know some people of nineteen who are much cleverer than you and Mary, and fifty million times nicer.'

'Oh, I say!' said Pierce. 'You've got us all wrong. I mean, Mary's terrified of *you*! She told me so. She says she feels all stiff and weird when you give her those icy looks. We'd both heard so much about you before we came – that you were one of these Wonder Girl Riders, and full of promise and a future queen of Wembley and all that, it quite put us off and we decided to squash you –'

'But I'm not!' I cried. 'I can't really ride for toffee, and when I saw your marvellous horses, and Mary said my pony was a sweet little thing –'

'Look here!' said Pierce. 'If you like, you can have a try on my horse tomorrow. Would you like to?'

'Rather!' I said.

'And can I try Black Boy? I think he's got a lovely action, and I'm not too heavy for him, and I don't think my feet will quite touch the ground. I say! Mary will be relieved that you've come unstuck. It's given her a pain in the neck trying to hold her own with you.'

To make a long story short, before the next day was over Mary, Pierce, and I were quite good friends.

# 18 - Chatton Show

'I'M looking forward to Saturday,' said Ann, as we rode happily homewards after a gallop on Neshbury Common. 'Up to yesterday I was scared stiff, and now I've changed right over and I'm dying for it. Isn't that weird?'

'It's the biggest thing we've ever entered for,' I said. 'Chatton Show.'

It was a year later than all the other events I have recorded in this book, and Ann and I were now thirteen and a half and experienced riders. We had several gymkhanas behind us, and both had certificates in a drawer at home, though I had never won a First.

The event we were talking about was the Chatton Show gymkhana which was to be held the following Saturday and was *the* event of the year. Not only were there classes for children but also for grown-ups, and the Open Jumping at Chatton attracted some of the most famous riders in England so we were longing to see it, apart from anything else.

Ann and I had both entered for everything.

'It was Susan Pyke's birthday yesterday,' said Ann, 'and she was fourteen. So that puts her out of the under-fourteens. All the better for us.'

'I'm sorry,' I said. 'I'd rather compete with her. If I could beat her in just one event I'd pass out with joy.'

'There's the under-sixteens events,' said Ann. 'She'll be in those.'

'Fat chance I have of winning anything in the under-sixteens,' I said, 'with people like Maureen Chase and Frank Stabley who ride at Richmond!'

'Maureen Chase is one of these fast women over timber,' said Ann, 'and they nearly always lose their heads and use their whips too much. One of the judges is Major Parkinson, and he simply hates whips and deducts marks for using them. I'm not even going to carry a riding stick; then I can't be tempted. If Seraphine doesn't know my hand and foot aids she jolly well ought to by now.'

'Black Boy's jumping pretty well,' I said. 'He's taken two Seconds for jumping, though one was at Ashbrow Farm which was only a small affair. And the other time I was competing against kids of about ten. I hadn't the slightest excuse for not getting a First.'

'Do you remember our first gymkhana together?' said Ann with a giggle. 'It was at Lentham Park, and La Blonde –'

'Goodness, yes!' I said. 'I got twenty-three faults in the jumping. It seems an age ago.'

'I *am* looking forward to Saturday,' said Ann enthusiastically, and I agreed, 'Same here.'

When we got to our cottage we found Martin there with the gymkhana schedule and we rushed to examine it.

'Oh!' I yelled. 'The riding class isn't under fourteen, it's fourteen and under, so we'll have Susan in it after all. I'm jolly glad, though of course I haven't a hope.'

'There's a sixteen-and-under riding class too,' said Ann. 'Bending, fourteen and under – ditto sixteen and under. Ditto, ditto, musical chairs. Open egg and spoon race! Gosh! Open? How weird! Do you suppose there'll be *men* riding in an egg and spoon race?'

'If there are,' said Martin, 'I pity them. I back you children every time for balancing eggs.'

'Look!' I said. 'There's only one children's jumping class. Sixteen and under. Clear round for Maureen Chase, obviously.'

But I was laughing when I said this, because I really had the gayest feeling about the whole gymkhana. I didn't expect anything, and therefore I was just going to enjoy the riding and have the time of my life, and Martin said that this was the ideal spirit for a gymkhana.

'I have got *just* a hope in the bending,' said Ann. 'Seraphine's developed a passion for it. I think she practises by herself when I'm not there, she's got so good lately.'

We shrieked with laughter at the thought of Seraphine solemnly practising bending by herself, in and out of the trees, and Martin said, 'Well, above all, don't go through the last two poles so quickly that you over-run and lose ground. Keep your head, and leave the bend to Seraphine; she knows her stuff. I must say, I've never seen a pony turn with such economy of space at the last pole. Let's hope she'll do it on the day.'

It was now getting late and Mummy had to come in and drive Ann and Martin off to their respective homes or we should have been discussing the gymkhana programme all night.

Ann was round at our cottage early on the day, and we spent the morning in an orgy of grooming, washing tails, and cleaning tack. It was a glorious day with a high blue sky and big white billowy clouds like feather beds, and a lively little wind blowing Black Boy's tail about. He looked lovely when I had finished him; his coat was like black satin and he arched his neck as though he knew how beautiful he was. I hugged him and gave him oats in my hand.

When we got to the Showground the band was playing, flags were flying, and large fat cattle were parading round and round. We rode in through the competitors' entrance, and made our way to the shade of the trees where the other children, looking so efficient, were leading their shining ponies up and down and putting finishing touches to what looked more perfect grooming than ours. I don't know how it is at gymkhanas, but however nice you think you look when you leave home everybody else seems to look so much better.

However we joined the others, and presently a steward came along and gave us our numbers. Ann was twenty-two and I was twenty-five. We fastened them on our backs, and then in rode Susan Pyke on another striking pony! This one was described as a roan, but quite honestly it was nearer rose-pink, and it was hogged and docked and had very long legs and looked as if it could win the Grand National.

'Hullo!' said Susan in a very friendly way. 'Hullo, Jill. Hullo, Ann. How do you like my Jupiter? He's a show jumper. Daddy said he wasn't going to make any mistake about my winning the jumping this time.'

'Well, his legs are most awfully long,' said Ann. 'I should think he'll just stride over the jumps.'

'I suppose you two have entered for everything,' said Susan. 'Well, I hope you'll have better luck than you had last season. Of course it's rather tough for you as beginners being up against anybody like Frank Stabley. He always takes the Firsts in the two riding classes.'

'Which is he?' I asked.

'Over there, on the chestnut. Number fourteen. Well, good luck.'

'Good luck,' we echoed.

Everybody was moving now to the collecting ring. The gymkhana was on a much bigger scale than anything I had ever entered for before, the ring, the grandstand, the judges, and many grown-up riders, but still I didn't have the needle. I just thought what a wonderful sight it was and how lucky I was to be part of it and to have a heavenly pony like Black Boy to ride. I wouldn't have changed him for any pony I saw on the field.

Presently the first class was called, and we were all riding quietly round the ring in the fourteen-and-under. It was a lovely feeling. Then the judges told us to trot and then to canter, and off we all went. I noticed how beautifully Black Boy was holding his head, and I had never known him pace so smoothly. Then I saw that Frank Stabley had been called in. The judge was calling another number, but I didn't take much notice until Ann, who was riding behind me, said in an excited voice, 'Go on in, Jill you idiot! Twenty-five – that's you!'

I couldn't believe it. As though in a dream I rode in and took second place, next to Frank Stabley. A girl I didn't know was third, and Susan Pyke fourth. Then the others lined up beyond.

Frank did a beautiful figure of eight. He dismounted and mounted, unsaddled and saddled again, walked and ran with his pony. It looked perfect to me. I did what was told me in a daze, thinking that every minute I should be sent down; but I wasn't. And five minutes later the judge was handing me a blue rosette and I was fastening it at Black Boy's ear. Second in the riding class!

I think it was the biggest thrill of my life as I galloped

madly round the ring with a blue certificate in my teeth, and from the tail of my eye caught sight of Mummy and Mrs Derry and the small Derry children and Martin and his father and mother, all sitting together and clapping like mad.

'Oh, jolly good!' shouted Ann enthusiastically as I joined her in the collecting ring. 'And did you see what happened? Susan lost her fourth place because that pink horse of hers dug his heels in and showed his teeth at the judge. Now you've got your ambition!'

So we all rode into the ring again for the sixteen-and-under, and this time we were up against some competition, including the famous Maureen Chase in full hunting kit. I don't know what kind of a pony Maureen usually rode, but this time she had foolishly chosen a wild-eyed bay that she could hardly hold in. At first she looked very striking, but after Comet – as he was called according to the programme – had run backwards into three other ponies, and given an exhibition of fly-catching, she was certainly 'out' so far as the judges were concerned.

A girl called Peach Morrison who was in our sixth form at school was first, I – to my amazement – was second again, Frank Stabley was third, and Ann was fourth and got the green 'highly commended'.

By now I was so happy that I didn't mind what else happened.

'I think the judges must be cockeyed,' I said to Ann.

'I've never seen you ride so well, Jill,' she said. 'There's something magic about you today.'

'I never enjoyed myself so much,' I said. 'Oh dear, I do hope Martin won't think I'm pot-hunting, because I'm not. He hates anything like that.'

The next event was the bending race. In my heat I

was lucky enough to get the outside position, which gives you more room, provided your pony doesn't mind the crowd. Black Boy didn't; he seemed to be chuckling as he threaded the poles and came thundering home to win me my heat. To my delight Ann won her heat also, and we raced in the final side by side. We thought Frank Stabley was a certain winner, but he got over-excited and missed out the third pole without realizing it, so he was disqualified, and I was first and Ann was second.

Then came the sixteen-and-under bending, and Ann actually was first in this and I was third, with a sixteen-year-old boy called Tom Jobling second.

By the time the Musical Chairs began we knew we were going to have fun. Black Boy always did love Musical Chairs and never had to be dragged into the ring, but fairly galloped up to a chair with me loping along beside him. Susan Pyke and I were left in together at the end, and finished up a dead heat by crashing down on the chair and breaking two legs off, so everybody roared and we had to do it again. Again we crashed into each other simultaneously, and had to run it off a third time. By now I was utterly breathless, so I left it to Black Boy who, defying the rose-pink roan, got me home just one second before Susan. So I got the first and she got the second. I went straight in for the senior event, but was out early. To my delight, Ann won third place in that.

The egg-and-spoon was lovely; grown-ups and children all in together. I won my heat, and was in the final with Maureen Chase, and a strange man, and my old friend, Mrs Darcy!

Maureen kept her egg on the spoon, but her nappy pony ran out and disappeared into the far distance, and that was the end of her.

I dropped my egg and thought I was finished, but when I went back for it I saw that Mrs Darcy had also dropped hers, and the man was nearly home. I thought it was a foregone conclusion, then there came a yell from the crowd. In handing the egg on the spoon to the judge, the man rider had dropped it!

Mrs Darcy and I were both up again by now; it was a neck-and-neck race between us, and she won by half a head. I was glad she was first; and I was second.

Next came the tea interval and I went to join Mummy and our friends who greeted me and Ann with slaps on the back.

'Nice work,' said Martin as we came up, and we both glowed a bit.

'Mine was just luck,' said Ann, 'but Jill's riding like a cyclops.'

'You mean, if she had two eyes she'd be riding like a centaur,' said Martin, and we all laughed as we munched our sandwiches and put away a lot of ice cream. Then we went to have a look at the ponies and made a fuss of them for doing so well, and we found them resting quietly in the shade of the trees and making soft little nickering noises of pleasure when they heard us speaking to them, and saw the handfuls of oats we held out to them.

# 19 – 'Jill's Gymkhana'

'WHAT lovely jumps!' said Ann.

'They look like precipices to me,' I remarked. 'But they are lovely, all the same.'

We were leaning over the railings to watch the first event after the interval which was the Open Jumping. I always think this event is the most wonderful thing in the world to watch; there is something utterly splendid about it, to see the tall, magnificent horses soar into the air under their skilful riders' touch, all in such harmony and effortless control. Everything around is beautiful too; the white painted jumps and the bright green field, the eager faces round the ring and the grandstand packed with people ready to cheer. And to think that there are actually people who never go to gymkhanas!

When number thirty-one was called we saw Mrs Darcy ride into the ring on a lovely lean grey called Martha, who I knew from my own experience was capable of anything if she could keep her temperament in control. This was one of Martha's good days, and she jumped a beautifully collected round, finishing with only one and a half faults.

'I think she's got a chance,' I said excitedly.

However, a strange man on a black hunter won first place with no faults, and a boy of twenty who we were told had won Firsts all over the country was second with one fault. To my joy, Mrs Darcy got third place, which was pretty good considering the competition, as there were nineteen entries.

The open event over, the stewards began to lower the jumps for the novice jumping. In this event I had the thrill of seeing my friend Angela jump a clear round on Inez, and everybody cheered like mad. In the end she tied for first place with a hunting man called Markham, who kept a lot of horses, and they jumped it off and Angela won! It was a great honour to have won a First in the novice-jumping at Chatton Show.

Then the jumps were lowered again, and this time it was US. So Ann and I rode round to the collecting ring, and we both had the feeling that our hearts were jumping about inside and doing gymkhanas on their own. In any case they say that if you don't have this feeling you are not much good.

There were twenty-six children competing, of all ages from twelve to sixteen; and there was the famous Maureen Chase looking cool and distant, and the famous Frank Stabley who I thought looked an awfully nice boy, and Susan Pyke, backing her pink horse into the others and getting black looks from everybody.

She kept saying, 'I can't help it. He's so full of spirit. You see, he's a show jumper, not just an *ordinary* pony' – and she gave all our 'ordinary' ponies very scornful glances.

'Well, you're *in*,' said Ann to Susan, as a boy called Peters came riding back to the ring and the megaphone called out 'Thirteen faults.' 'So you can let your charger charge!'

All eyes were on Susan as she made a spectacular entrance; but I didn't like the way the roan pawed the ground, or the look in his eye. He had a silly, wild look,

not the sensible clever look of a pony who is going to d‹
any good at jumping.

He went straight at the first jump, which was the bush
before Susan was ready, and nearly unseated her; how‹
ever he cleared the jump with inches to spare, and a gir
next to me said, 'Some show jumper!'

Susan was now obviously trying to collect her pony,
but he refused to be collected. He went full tilt at the nex
jump, which was the gate, soared into the air, bucked i‹
mid-air, got his feet in a knot, and sent Susan flying si›
yards. She landed with a thud, and the pink horse, havin‹
done his stuff, ran right out of the ring neighing at the to›
of his voice.

Susan sat there on the ground, quite openly weeping
for all to see. Two stewards went and helped her up, an‹
there was obviously nothing the matter with her, s‹
presently she landed back among us looking very low.

'Serves her jolly well right!' said a girl next to me. 'Sh‹
always ruins every gymkhana for everybody else. The›
ought to disqualify her permanently.'

Susan could not help hearing this remark, and Ann
who was soft-hearted went across to her and said kindly
'It was jolly hard luck, Susan.'

'Oh, thank you, Ann,' said Susan, in a very humbl‹
and heartfelt tone, quite different from her usual bragging
one.

Meanwhile Maureen Chase had gone in and done a‹
efficient but uninspiring round, to finish up with tw‹
faults, and a boy called Michael Grant was making the
crowd roar by sending everything flying.

Then it was Ann's turn, and I knew she would enjo›
herself because she didn't expect much from Seraphine
To my surprise – and hers – Seraphine jumped the roun‹

of her life, finishing with only four faults, and she and Ann looked so pretty and graceful jumping that the crowd clapped and cheered like mad, and the judges all smiled with pleasure at Ann as she rode so neatly and nicely off.

Frank Stabley had very bad luck. He took four jumps perfectly, but just as he approached the triple bar a dog fight broke out in the crowd only about five yards away. Frank's pony reared, and then being quite upset gave him three refusals. I was awfully sorry about this as Frank certainly was an excellent jumper.

Then my number was called. As I rode into the ring I had the strangest feeling of being most awfully happy, and I could tell that Black Boy was feeling the same way. I whispered into his ear, 'Now, angel, don't bother about all those people. We're just jumping for fun, like we do at home, and it's going to be heavenly.'

He arched his neck, and looked both proud and serious, and so at a collected canter we approached the first jump. I only had to whisper, 'Hup!' and the next minute we were over, so smoothly that I had hardly felt him rise. I knew then that he was going to do it! I knew that he and I were just like one single person. So we took the gate, and then the wall, and then – with only the slightest pause – the tricky in-and-out. We were coming up to the triple bar now. I stroked his neck, and whispered, 'Don't rush, boy. Do just as I tell you.' I had forgotten the crowd and everything except those three white bars ahead, sparkling in the sunshine.

'Now!' I said suddenly. 'Hup!'

And then I did feel him soar. I felt him gather his legs up in that lovely careful way of his, and I felt the rush of the wind on my face, and then I could hardly believe it for we were on the ground again and everybody was clapping and I wasn't quite conscious as I patted him and couldn't say a word as he carried me out of the ring and the megaphones blared, 'Clear round.'

Was this really me, or was I dreaming? Surely jumping a clear round in the under-sixteens at Chatton Show was the sort of thing that *could* only happen in a dream? But I came round when some of my friends began to thump me on the back until my tie nearly flew off, and I gasped, 'Well, it's nothing really. About six other people are sure to jump clear rounds.'

But strangely enough nobody else did, and presently three of us were called in. I was first, a boy called Lloyd was second with one fault, and Maureen Chase was third with two. After I had received my red rosette I was told that I must also go up to the grandstand to receive the Hopley Challenge Cup, to be held for a year. So with a scarlet face and hands that felt like hams I took this large silver cup in my arms, and muttered something like 'Oh, thanks!' to somebody in tweeds who I afterwards found out was Lord Hopley. And then my at-no-times-particularly-graceful exit was competely ruined when I dropped the black ebony base of the thing, which fell on the ground with a resounding thud and had to be rescued by a steward, while howls of derision mingled with the cheers of the populace.

One place where I simply dare not look was the front row of the stand where Mummy and my own friends were sitting. I let myself go in the usual wild gallop round the ring; and when I came to the exit, there they all were.

'Good kid,' was all that Martin said. And Mummy added, 'Not bad at all, Jill, but why on earth did you have to drop that thing?'

'There's nothing left now but the Grand Parade,' said Martin. 'Hand Black Boy over to Bob here, who'll give him a rub down and you scoot off and have a wash and brush-up.'

'Jill Crewe,' said Ann solemnly, coming up to me, 'do you realize that you've taken three Firsts, three Seconds, and a Third!'

'You mean Black Boy has,' I said. 'I wish I was as nice a person as he is a pony.'

So with my cap, boots, and jodhpurs brushed, and my tie re-tied, I rejoined Black Boy who under Bob's skilful hand looked as if he was made of patent leather. Then headed by the local band we joined in the Grand Parade – in which everything that has won Firsts in the Show marches slowly round and round the ring – and Black Boy gave me quite a look when he found he had to do a collected walk behind a lot of fat cows and dairy turnouts.

At last it was all over. As I rode out I passed Frank Stabley and his father, and they smiled at me and I heard Frank say, 'Look, Dad, that's the girl who won everything. Pretty good, what?'

And Mr Stabley said, 'They say that Martin Lowe trained her, so you'd *expect* something.'

I was frightfully happy, but I didn't feel the least bit cocky or conceited, because I knew that I'd had a lot of luck and that this was the sort of day which only comes to a person once in a lifetime. And I have written this book to show what a quite ordinary person can do with a quite ordinary pony, if he or she really cares about riding.

As we all left the Showground together, there stood Mrs Darcy and gave me a gay salute.

'Well, well, well!' she said in her loud, hearty way. 'It certainly has been Jill's gymkhana!'

And with those magic words ringing in my ears, turned my pony happily towards home.

But the wonders of this great day were not qui ended. Mummy of course had gone on ahead in th Derrys' car, and when I reached our gate I saw he standing at the door waiting for me, and looking ver excited.

'Oh, Jill,' she cried. 'What do you think?'

'If anything else nice happens I shall burst,' I said.

'Well, prepare to burst,' said Mummy. 'When I g home there was a letter on the mat to say that a firm c American publishers want to buy the American rights c *all* my books, and they're going to pay me a simpl stunning sum for them. We'll have money to spare, Jil so if you'd like it, we can move into a much bigger hous and buy new furniture and things.'

'Jolly good!' I said. 'Congrats, Mummy.'

I went upstairs, picturing all the cute little America children simply wallowing in the squalid adventures o Winnie and Terry and the Fairy-of-Little-Duties-Daily Done and the rest. I went into my room and pushe everything off the chest of drawers and put the three re rosettes and the three blue rosettes and the yellow one and the certificates that went with them, and the cup and the ebony base that I'd dropped, and the prize mone that was all going to be spent on Black Boy, all down o the white runner. And the weirdest choky feeling cam in my throat. I went and looked out of my funny littl window, and there was the lane and Black Boy standing patiently where I had left him with his reins hitched ove the fence waiting for me to go and feed him and turn hin into his nice orchard.

Gosh, how choky I felt!

I threw my crash cap on the bed and went charging downstairs.

'Mummy,' I said. 'I don't want to go away from the cottage and live in another house. We don't have to, do we? It's been such fun here, and all the *nicest* things have happened.'

And suddenly a kind of light broke all over her face.

'I don't want to leave either, Jill,' she said. 'Let's stay!'

'Oh, wizard!' I said.

Then I had an idea.

'I say, Mummy,' I said, 'if you really do want to spend some money, what about enlarging the stable? I mean, I hate to think of it, but soon Black Boy is going to be too small for me, and I shall need something about fifteen-two. And' – I added as an afterthought, my plans soaring into the region of the grand and spacious – 'if we could run to about three loose boxes, you could have a horse and learn to ride too. Think it over while I go and mix the oats.'